Autumn's Ghost

The Fantasy Maker Series

Cricket Rohman

Cover Design by Sweet 'N Spicy Designs

ISBN: 978-1-7355672-1-1

Ebook ISBN: 978-1-7355672-0-4

This book is dedicated to parents who supervise their children as they enjoy the fun aspects of the Halloween holiday. Enjoy and be safe.

Acknowledgments

A big thank you to:

Jaycee DeLorenzo, my formatter and cover designer extraordinaire.

My editor, Michelle Kowalski, for her tenacious attention to detail.

Jerry Gallegos, who insists that I step away from the computer now and then. He is my go-to guy when it comes to equine questions and other manly topics.

The real Cliff Rosario for finding the way to lessen my pain . . . it's complicated.

My readers. Without you, the joy of creating fictional stories would be greatly diminished.

Chapter One

Autumn

I parked my white BMW in the library's small parking lot and stepped out into the heat and humidity. Even though fall was just around the corner, the weather in Cape Coral, Florida, could make a woman's hair and makeup wilt like month-old lettuce forgotten in the bottom of the fridge. Fortunately, I had thick, low-maintenance hair, and I was just a mascara and lip-gloss gal on most days. Today was one of those days. Knowing I was running behind schedule, I hurried into the library.

"Sorry I'm a little late. Traffic crawled slower than usual across the Cape Coral Bridge," I said, patting the dampness from my face with a soft, pink handkerchief. The library was old, and so was its AC unit. So, though much cooler than outside, the faces of my ten book club friends glistened a bit.

The ladies looked at me, merely shrugged, smiled semi-hidden smiles, and raised their eyebrows.

"What's up? I was only ten minutes late. Somebody say something." No explanation was forthcoming.

"We need to vote on our next book," said Lu, the group's senior member. *"The House of Seven Gables* by Nathaniel Hawthorn has been nominated. Are there any objections to this choice?"

My hand went up immediately. All eyes turned toward me, though I knew none were surprised by my objection. They knew me well. "But it's a classic," chimed in several voices. One of the club's rules was that it required a unanimous vote for a book to be the chosen one.

"Yes, and it's a bit dark and frightening, don't you think?" I said. "October is just a month away, and I'd prefer to read something that focused more on fall fun. You know, colorful leaves, apples, pumpkins, or maybe a cute Halloween romantic comedy."

No one was buying into my idea. The group liked to read and discuss mysteries, thrillers, historical romance, or books containing challenging content and on one of the bestseller lists.

"Good grief. Just because your name is Autumn doesn't mean we should select a book about the coming season," said JoAnne, the one all-too-frank member of the group.

That did it. A ruckus began. Everyone spoke at once, voicing their disapproval of JoAnne's comment and my request for a cute Halloween book.

Lu slammed the current book down on the table, which got our attention, the librarian's too. "Is there a problem here?" the librarian asked, now standing in the doorway of the small room we always reserved for our bi-weekly meetings.

Silently, we all shook our heads, embarrassed at our noisy, inexcusable conduct.

"No, we're fine," Lu said. "I dropped my book, and everyone chattered about my clumsiness. We are so sorry for our boisterous behavior. It won't happen again." We all nodded as if we agreed with the little white lie.

The librarian gave the group a suspicious look and then began to back out of the doorway. "Just keep it down, Ok?"

We all nodded and murmured that we'd be quiet, and then sat back down to resume our discussion. Not ready to give up, I had an idea. "Since we haven't finished reading *West With Giraffes,* why not spend the time between now and our next meeting in two weeks searching for additional possibilities to choose from?"

No one objected to that suggestion. Most of the members gave either an approving nod or thumbs up. Before long, the meeting was back on track, and the discussion about the giraffe's incredible journey continued.

Glancing at the clock, I noticed the book club's meeting was about to adjourn. Several women had begun to pack up their books and notes already.

"I promise to bring a substantial list of books to our next meeting that I am sure every member will enjoy, including me." I smiled, looking directly toward Allison, my best friend, who'd convinced me to join this book club.

"Shouldn't we tell her?" Allison said, glancing around the table at the others who were already standing, poised to leave.

Her question brought a wave of silence, and everyone sat back down.

"I know I was a few minutes late; did I miss something?" I hadn't a clue as to the meaning of Allison's question.

When no one else spoke up, Allison continued. "It didn't happen today, Autumn. We had a meeting without you a few weeks ago."

My initial thoughts were filled with anger, then worry. Did they plan to exclude me from this club just because I occasionally disagreed with the others' choices?

"Tell her. She has a right to know." Allison spoke firmly. "If you won't tell her, I will."

"Fine. I'll make it quick." Lu raised her arms, let out a heavy sigh, and looked directly at me. "Here goes. We all know that autumn is your favorite time of the year. We also know that you have high hopes to make photography and photojournalism a career and become your life's work."

There was nothing quick about Lu's delivery of information. My foot tapped the floor while my fingers drummed on the table. I remained clueless and more worried than before.

"Allison found—" Lu started.

"Yes, I found an interesting article in one of my magazines offering an opportunity for a deserving person. We barely made the deadline. Long story short, we nominated you to receive the prize."

Was this a joke? A prank? "What kind of opportunity? What kind of prize?" I asked, hoping it might be a camera—my phone took great pictures, but I've wanted a real camera for quite a while. Still, I doubted the authenticity of this too-good-to-be-true opportunity. Allison was not above kidding around.

JoAnne jumped into the explanation. "It is a fantasy vacation. We requested the location be in New Hampshire during the best fall color days. A perfect time to capture some good photos."

"Don't get too excited yet. I'm sure there were lots of other deserving folks nominated too," added Lu.

"True," said Allison. "But when we learned they would only contact the winner, I felt you should know ahead of time just in case you are the winner."

"I don't know what to say," I tingled with anticipation and gratitude. "Win or lose, thank you so much for thinking of me."

"You can thank us if and when you win this fantasy vacation," said JoAnne. "Being a rich gal, the odds are not in your favor."

"Shut up, JoAnne!" Allison said, scowling.

Lu cleared her throat, stood up, and announced, "Our time for today is up. See you in two weeks. Happy reading, everyone."

Heading to our cars, I turned toward Allison and gave her the call-me hand sign. She signaled back with a thumbs up.

On the drive home, a perplexing thought mingled with the joy I felt from today's successful meeting. What had JoAnne called the prize? A *fantasy* vacation? Did that mean it was merely virtual make-believe? A fanciful notion? Some pie-in-the-sky daydream? I had read several books in the fantasy genre, and though I enjoyed those books, I wanted no part of those fantasy plots in my real life.

As Mother and I sat at the waterfront restaurant enjoying the slight breeze and the sound of the Gulf's gently lapping blue water, a seagull swooped low, causing us to duck from its trajectory. Mother laughed and said, "Wouldn't you know that the one time I didn't wear a hat, I'd be accosted by a bird."

I looked up, chuckling to express that I'd heard her comment.

"You're mighty quiet today, Autumn," she said. "What's on your mind?"

"Just thinking about applying to grad school."

"Oh, why would you want to do that? We can give you everything you'll ever need."

My mother was clueless when it came to being anything other than the wife of a wealthy man.

"That may well be, Mother. But what I want is a career in photojournalism. I doubt you can give me that."

"We'll discuss this at another time. Today our topic is your birthday. How about a nice lunch in Paris or Prague? You name it, and I'll make it happen."

My shoulders slumped. No matter what my age, nothing ever changed. They still treated me like a China doll.

"Oh, Mother, I've been to Paris and Prague. You and Father have taken me all over the world. This year, I want to go somewhere here in the States . . . by myself."

"You know your father would never allow that."

I was a good girl and had always done exactly what my parents wanted. But I could no longer hide the fact that I craved freedom and independence. I dreamed of dancing with a handsome man without my father close by watching our every move. He couldn't keep me tucked away in a gilded cage forever. Could he? I loved fairy tales but never wished to be Rapunzel.

The awkward silence dashed away with the arrival of

our food. On each plate lay a giant lobster. Not my choice; it was never my choice. Either Mother or Father always ordered for me. I disliked crunching up the creature's exoskeleton before eating it. I wanted to shout out to the world that I was an intelligent, twenty-two-year-old woman who was more than ready to spread her wings. But as a family, we never made a spectacle of ourselves in public or in private, so the only shouting took place within my head.

I tried to hide my disgust as I picked at the sea creature on my plate. Mother devoured hers long before I had consumed one of the claws.

"Waiter," she called, snapping her fingers. "Could you please crack open my daughter's lobster? It is taking her far too long."

The waiter obliged, likely knowing my mother was a big tipper. He also gave me a special smile indicating that he understood my situation. At least that's how I saw it. I actually enjoy the taste of lobster, though I'm not fond of the process involved. It was the lack of choice that left the bitterness in my mouth. I left much of the sea creature on my plate.

After we finished eating and the plates were cleared from the table, Mother picked up the conversation right where we'd left off. "At the very least, tell me about something you'd love to see or do, and I'll put together a birthday surprise for you."

I needed no time to think, already knowing my answer. "I've been all over the world, but I've never been to New England, and I hear that is the best place for a photographer to be in October. I want to experience and photograph all the colors of those famous fall leaves."

"Hmm. Looking at leaves? Interesting, though a bit boring. That doesn't sound like a birthday celebration suitable for a member of our family."

"Well, that's what I want. If the photos I shoot there are good enough, I could include them in my application to one of the schools of photojournalism."

"Let's keep this conversation to ourselves for now. No need to get your father concerned about your wild ideas," her mother said, completely dismissing her.

That was not the reaction I'd hoped for though should have expected. I thought with each passing year my parents would lighten up when it came to me living my life. It seemed this was not the year for that.

Mother caught the waiter's attention and said, "Check, please." She never again mentioned the trip to New England, but, in her defense, she had said she'd put together a surprise for my birthday.

Ranger

I returned to base flying one of the Forest Service's Air Tractor AT-802s. I loved my job with the White Mountain Forest Service but preferred the groundwork portion of forest health and wildlife care. I'd rather fly my own plane for fun whenever I took some time off, which I rarely did.

Today I'd been called to assist with a small fire. By the time I arrived, the fire had grown considerably. In September and October, the area was often dry, and this year was no exception. I was relieved to see a crew of about twelve firefighters already there. I helped them by delivering water drops over and over from the plane. By mid-afternoon, the ground crew and I were able to head back to our respective home bases.

"See you next time, Ranger," one of the crew shouted and waved from the ground.

"Copy that," I called back, though I doubt he could hear me.

I couldn't wait to get this plane on the ground and put away. A better-than-nothing, uncomfortable bed and a cold beer were calling to me. Some day, I'd take the time to find a real home that I could call my own. Until then, the small Forest Service cabin would have to do. If the truth be known, I liked it, though a better bed would be nice.

I sat on the porch of the one-bedroom cabin I called home for now. *Fall. I loved the crisp air and watching the leaves as their colors cycled from one shade to the next.* My breathing slowed; my eyes grew heavy. The day's work had taken its toll, and now the silence—except for a few squirrels chattering and dashing around hoarding nuts for the long winter they'd face—lulled me into a dream-like state of mind.

Pleasant memories flooded my thoughts of hiking through the forest, leaves crunching underfoot, and the aroma of the soil welcoming those leaves as they slowly returned to be one with the earth. I didn't mind the task of raking leaves back home in North Andover when I was still a boy, and I loved smelling the spicy apple cider my mother had simmering on the stove. I laughed, thinking about the first time I was allowed to carve a face on the family pumpkin. It looked strange. Not scary, not funny, not cute. It was just plain ugly.

My laughable jack-o-lantern memory quickly vanished, overtaken by visions of my distressing childhood experience—the year Halloween became the worst day of my life.

Chapter Two

Autumn

Heading down the hallway toward the front door, I called out, "Bye, Mother. I'm going to book club now." Participating in book club was the one activity my over-protective parents always allowed. My father even encouraged it. After all, what harm could come to a pretty young woman at the local library in the middle of the day?

Mother poked her head around the corner of the main living room. "How's my favorite season doing today?"

"I'm fine, Mother." Then I mumbled softly, "Your childish, daily question is getting old."

"Check the mail on your way out, please. I'm going to sit by the pool to work on my tan."

"Of course." I shook my head at the silliness of my mother's comment. Her skin was already a beautiful, dark cinnamon color, which did not come from the sun. It came from her Cuban ancestry. I released a deep sigh. Mother had time to work on her unneeded tan but no time to arrange my birthday request. I popped several Tic Tacs into my mouth to mask the bitter taste I felt.

With a carefully researched list of books in one hand, I opened the family's ostentatious mailbox located by the front entrance with the other. I'd subscribed to a photography magazine weeks ago, and every day I hoped to find it there. Today would not be my lucky day. Flipping quickly through the envelopes noting that most were bills for my parents, I paused and stared at the only one addressed to me.

I rarely received any mail worth opening, let alone eye-catching, unusual-looking mail. The envelope was made from heavy cream-colored stock and was fancier than most wedding invitations. My name looked as if it were hand-written with golden ink. There was no return address, but on the back of the envelope embossed in gold were three large letters: T F M.

When the hall clock chimed, announcing the time, I shoved the fancy envelope—my envelope—into my book bag and left the rest of the mail in the mailbox. I could not be late for two meetings in a row. This club limited its membership, and I could not afford to lose the only solo outing I was always granted—no questions asked.

No traffic issues today. I arrived at the library's parking lot in record time. Before I'd even locked the BMW with its key fob, my best friend pulled up next to me.

"Hey, Autumn. Where've you been? On one of your frequent rich girl trips with mommy and daddy?" Allison said breathlessly, hurrying toward me.

Those would have been fighting words if anyone else had said them, but it was Allison. The two of us often bantered and teased each other. Allison was a rich girl too, although the only travel her parents took part in occurred on their yacht. Sometimes they'd let her stay home when they went sailing. I envied her days of unbridled freedom.

"No, Father has some new clients keeping him busy right now, and Mother is working on her tan again."

We giggled and hurried inside the library.

JoAnne brought treats today—a bowl full of individually wrapped candy and cookies shaped like pumpkins. She handed everyone a tiny trick-or-treat bag and said, "Dig in!" And we all did with more joyful noise than a library should have. This group of women could be fun once in a while.

A few minutes later, Lu called for our gathering to come to order. She was quite the taskmaster, often treating our little book club as if it were some big corporate board meeting. "Let's begin by sharing our lists of books that we might like to read next. Then we'll vote."

Only three women offered ideas. I dug into my book bag for my list, but more than my list came out. In my rush to make sure I arrived on time, I'd forgotten about my mail. The gold embossed envelope now lying on the table created an unusual hush in the small meeting room. No cookies crunched, no candy wrappers crinkled, but every pair of eyes stared at the beautiful, unopened envelope.

"Open it, Autumn. Come on. We all want to know what's inside," said Allison.

Everyone nodded in agreement. After all, they were part of what I could only assume at this moment was something about the contest. They wrote and mailed in the form nominating me for, for . . . some kind of prize. The prize part was still a little vague.

"Open the damn envelope," JoAnne said, showing her impatience. "You must have won something. No one would put bad news in a flashy envelope like that."

"Good point. Okay. Here goes." I opened that envelope with the utmost care, first lifting the golden seal on the back, then gently removing what appeared to be a letter written on parchment paper. I began to read. My lips moved, though I made no sound as tears welled up in my eyes. Lu handed me a tissue as a drop or two trickled down my cheeks.

"Maybe it was bad news or at least not good news," the women chattered back and forth.

"What's the matter, Autumn? You can tell us," Allison's tone showed concern. "We all knew it was a long shot and the odds were against winning."

I looked up from the letter, hesitating. Then whispered, "I won."

All the women spoke at once with their comments.

"You won?"

"Don't keep us in suspense."

"What did you win?"

"Is it from the application we sent in?"

Still trying to take it all in, not ready to discuss the letter, I went around to every book club member and gave each one a hug before returning to my seat. Allison brought me some water, and JoAnne placed another pumpkin cookie in front of me.

"The letter speaks of the wonderful words written by all of you nominating me for an experience involving photography. But it gets better. They are flying me to New Hampshire on October 5th, all expenses paid, to photograph those glorious leaves during the peak of fall colors. The tickets, an itinerary, and a Sony A6500 camera with several lenses will arrive in two or three days."

The quiet little meeting room filled once again with joyful noise—applause, whoops, and hollers—until the librarian stood in the doorway, giving us the quiet-inducing finger sign. I suppose it could have been worse. Did I really just have that thought? At least I didn't say it out loud.

"Well, I've got a quiet finger for you too, but it won't be—"

"JoAnne," Lu said sternly in the nick of time, "pass around the cookies." Then, looking at the librarian with a penitent expression, she added, "We just received some extraordinary news and got a little carried away. We're so sorry. It won't happen again."

Everyone's eyes were busy staring at the floor, the bowl of candy, or the window, anything but each other to avoid laughing out loud.

"Here's the plan," said Lu. "Autumn will tell us everything she knows about her upcoming trip. We'll take a few more minutes to ask questions if we have any, and we will decide on our next book. All in favor?"

With only a few club members rolling their eyes, all agreed to Lu's plan.

"I'll know more when I see the itinerary, and I'll email everyone with the details. All I know today is approximately where I'm going and when."

Allison knew my parents and their over-the-top protectiveness and asked, "Will you be traveling alone?"

"It looks that way. I'm the winner, and there was no mention of bringing a companion. I suppose we'll know for sure when the plane ticket or tickets arrive."

We'd used up most of our allotted time at the library, so we chose a book with little discussion. To my surprise, the group agreed on *The Bake Shop at Pumpkin and Spice*. I didn't mind missing out; I'd be knee-deep in fall colors before the next meeting.

Allison and I walked out together. "Go ahead and say what's on your mind. I'm pretty sure I know what you're thinking."

"Well, you lived at home the entire time you attended college. Your dad will never let you travel far away by yourself."

"I've traveled all over the world. I know how to do that."

"Uh, huh, with your mom and dad." Suddenly, Allison had a mischievous grin on her face. "I'd bet money that they'll try to stop you from going. So, what you need is an escape plan."

"Now you're talking. Sounds good, but we don't have much time to figure out that plan," I said, feeling brave for a brief moment. But did I really like the sound of that?

Ranger

I didn't mind that I worked a 5-day week, was on call 24/7, and rarely had a full day off. I'd outlived most of my family, so I faced no holiday or birthday demands anymore. My friends worked for the Forest Service too, so I saw them at meetings, disasters, and the occasional social event. The days of disappointing loved ones due to my recurring absences were long gone.

Now, I relaxed in front of the small fire ring in the clearing by my cabin. So far today, I had received no emergency calls. Although this unusual situation seemed too good to be true, I permitted myself to enjoy it. Returning inside the cabin, I retrieved three items to assist in my enjoyment of this peaceful afternoon: a warm jacket, my guitar, and an ice-cold beer tucked within a forest green koozie.

Sitting on my homemade chair—a modified tree stump—I mindlessly strummed my guitar, sipped my beer, and watched a red fox staring at me a mere five yards away. I stared back. The fox sat down, and since I had an audience, I continued playing my guitar.

This phenomenon brought a smile to my face and might have gone on for quite a while if the noise of an approaching vehicle had not jarred the peaceful wildlife moment. The fox dashed away but not without glancing back at me a few times.

A large, yellow van headed toward me much too fast. Its arrival was odder than the absence of emergency calls or the appearance of the fox. A delivery? Out here? Perhaps. But neither FedEx, USPS, nor UPS would drive all the way out to this old, remote cabin. I stood as a man jumped from the van holding a large envelope.

"Are you Ranger?" he asked.

"Yes."

"Then this is for you," the man said, holding out the envelope.

"Who is it from? And why are you *here*? All deliveries should be left at the Forest Service's main office."

"I can't answer your questions. My orders were to

deliver this envelope directly into your hands. Nothing else would do. Sure glad you were here today. I've stopped by two other times."

"Why didn't you leave a note?"

"Couldn't do that either. Have a good rest of your day, sir."

The man got back in his van and sped away. I stared at the front and the back of the envelope and shook my head. Was this some kind of joke? *To Ranger—The good-looking ranger in the White Mountain National Forest* were the only words there. No postmark and no return address. I hesitated to open it even though I could not think of a single soul that wished me harm. Still, the van, the driver, this envelope amounted to a whole lot of weirdness. *Am I overreacting?*

Not wanting to take any chances, I stepped back to my stump chair by the fire, ready to toss the worrisome envelope in and watch it burn, when the red fox caught my attention again. It had returned, but why? I hoped it wasn't sick.

"Hey, little buddy. You gave this piece of mail a reprieve." I liked having someone—or something—to talk to way out here deep in the forest. The fox tilted its head just like a dog might. I had always wanted a dog of my own, but I knew that would never happen because I was rarely at home. Today was a notable exception.

"Oh, what the heck." Curiosity won out, and I tore open this piece of mystery mail. Staring down at the single sheet of paper, I struggled to make sense of the words on the page. My failed efforts merely angered me. I crushed that paper and was about to chuck into the fire when a huge hawk swooped down toward the small fox.

I jumped up, startling the fast-moving bird. Luckily, its talons had not yet grasped its prey. As it left the area, it flew so close to my head that the whooshing sound of the hawk's wings was unmistakable. *That was a close one.*

Sitting back down, I noticed the fox had scooted closer to me and my chair. "I saved your life, you know, and what did you do? You gave this odd letter that I don't even want another chance." The fox came a little closer. "I am not going to feed you. So get that thought out of your foxy little mind. Feeding a wild animal like you is illegal and could lead you to danger, resulting in a shorter life," I said more to myself than the fox. "I'm going to call you Red. No law against that."

Back to the letter. Slowly, methodically, I uncrumpled the paper and then flattened it with my hands and read every word. It wouldn't take long.

TO: The White Mountain Ranger
WHAT: The reading of your uncle's will
WHEN: October 5 @ 10 AM
WHERE: 1214 W Suttner Street, New Haven, Connecticut
WHY: Your presence is required as per the will

I remained speechless for a while, then began talking to Red. "As a kid, I'd been told once that I had an uncle, but I can't recall his name. It seems he didn't know my name either. But he knew I existed." The more I mulled over the letter, a new thought came to mind, and I wondered who thought I was good-looking. Surely, not this unidentified uncle. We'd never met. But who?

Autumn

The time flew by; today was the day. "Our escape plan worked," I said, strolling with Allison toward Gate 5 at the Southwest Florida International Airport.

We did have a decent plan for the first two days of my 10-day vacation, which was awarded to me by something or someone called The Fantasy Maker. Apparently, a contest was held several times each year, awarding one person with an all-expenses paid dream vacation. It was truly a dream come true in more ways than one.

I wished Allison were going with me. That was our original plan—we'd each chipped in to purchase her plane ticket, but she backed out. I still wasn't sure why, but I'd find out someday.

"Tell me again the basics of your trip. I need to know exactly where you are and that you are doing Ok in case I get cornered and threatened with torture if I don't talk."

"No worries. My parents are strict, but I'm pretty sure they're not into torture," I laughed, and Allison joined in. "But lay low those first two days. My mother still thinks we are traveling together."

"Here," I said as I handed her a piece of paper. "I wrote down all the basics we'd discussed. You won't need to memorize that first day. I'm flying to Boston, where I'll have a forty-five-minute layover. After that, they'll fly me to the Lebanon Municipal Airport in New Hampshire, where I'll be whisked away in a limo to the Sugar Lane Inn. You also have a copy of the day trips planned for me as part of my fantasy vacation. Though, there was a side note stating that updates might occur."

As I packed for the trip, Allison and I had gone over my checklist for must-haves: warm clothing, my favorite toiletries, and a blank journal for recording everything I saw, did, or photographed. I'd stashed $500 in my cross-body bag for emergencies even though I'd been assured that anything I desired during my vacation would be paid for. The word "anything" had been underlined.

The third day—the day I planned to inform my mother where I was—would be tough.

"What's the worst thing that could happen?" asked Allison.

"I don't know. I've never lied to my parents or misbehaved before."

Allison burst out laughing again. "Then you've got a lot of catching up to do, girl."

"Flight 5261 to Boston is now boarding. Have your tickets ready please."

"I guess this is it," I said giving Allison a hug.

"Have a wonderful time, and be sure to call and tell me all about New Hampshire's fall leaves."

With butterflies fluttering in my belly, I got in line to board the plane.

Martin

The Fantasy Maker was well aware of the odd choice we'd just made. Typically, those replying to an advertisement announcing an opportunity to win a Fantasy Vacation entered the contest themselves. This was the first time we chose the winner from a nomination sent in by friends.

"Stop pacing, Martin. Autumn's trip may be the easiest fantasy to implement since the inception of my magnanimous project."

"I hope you're right. No matter how well-planned and executed, some of our past endeavors contained glitches."

"This young woman is not looking for love, so we're only dealing with one person's vacation. Don't you see the simplicity, the beauty of it all, Martin?"

"Yes, I understand that part, but this time our recipient is a rich young woman, born sipping from a proverbial silver spoon. She's got everything a woman could want."

"Ah, but she doesn't. What she needs most is missing. She desires freedom to live her life, to spread her wings. The nominators agreed that her greatest wish was to become a photojournalist, beginning with taking pictures of New England's world-famous fall leaves. She deserves our intervention, Martin."

"Yes, ma'am. I'm on it."

Chapter Three

Ranger

"Ranger's got a girlfriend," the guys chanted obnoxiously as I conducted my pre-flight check. I was allowed to keep my private plane with the other Forest Service planes. The chanting was followed by much laughter and non-stop teasing.

"We listened to your comments about your new friend, the red-headed fox. Nothing wrong with having a girlfriend," said James, his best friend.

"Yeah," added Mike, one of the fire crew. "It's about time."

I shook my head as I climbed into my plane. "You guys heard wrong. Yes, a red fox, the four-legged animal, has taken an interest in me and the cabin." I started the engine and shouted my parting words. "Got to pick up a few things and attend a meeting in New Haven. I'll be back before the sky goes black. Stay away from my fox."

I enjoyed getting the last laugh as I taxied out to the short runway.

"You're late," said the stranger as he rose stiffly from his creaking chair.

"Couldn't be helped," I explained. "Had some unusual headwinds, and this office was hard to find."

"Yeah. I had trouble too. Let's get started."

The man had trouble finding his own office? That was an odd thing to say. The dingy little office reeked of stale smoke. I hoped this meeting would be quick.

"Wait. Who are you, and where is everybody?"

The man reached out his hand and said, "I'm Buck Johnson, a friend and the executor of your uncle's estate."

"You're not an attorney?" I asked.

"Nope. Just a friend. Your uncle didn't trust attorneys."

"I didn't know I had an uncle. I don't recall anyone ever mentioned him. On my father's or mother's side?"

"Don't know the answer. Let's move on. Anyway, we're all here. Just you and me. I do have a question for you before we officially begin."

"Ok. Sure."

"What is your legal name? All I had was your title. The only thing your uncle remembered about you was that you were a ranger with the White Mountain Forest Service."

Too deep in thought, I didn't answer right away, but now the unusual wording on the envelope made a little more sense.

"My title and my first name are the same. I'm Ranger W. Lee, and I'm pleased to meet you, Buck Johnson."

Buck let out a hearty laugh. "Well, don't that beat all? Hey, you want a beer?"

"Sorry. Can't do that. I'll be flying my plane back up to New Hampshire in a few hours."

"Ok. Then, we'd better get down to business."

Buck explained that my late uncle gave away all of his belongings during the last few months of his life. He contributed to several charities, and recently, they benefitted even more from his death. There were just two items and one person left to bequeath them to. For reasons that had yet to be explained, that person was me.

"What items are we discussing here?"

"His old country estate. It's a large house with many rooms, but it does need some work." Buck handed me a sheet of paper.

The house's address caught my eye immediately. "A big old, New England house, and it's not too far from my work. Sure sounds interesting, almost like winning the lottery."

Could this be a joke or some kind of a setup?

Nothing about this situation seemed legit. It sounded too good to be true.

I watched as Buck took a manila envelope from his desk's center drawer. "Oh, I do have a few more questions. Since you were friends with my uncle, I assume you'll know the answer but more importantly, I hope you don't mind that I ask it. When and how did my uncle die?"

Buck sighed. His lips tightened as he scratched his balding head. "It's sad, but he knew it was coming. He was okay with that. The emphysema, the lung cancer, and then his weakening heart. About two weeks ago, he just went to sleep in the barn with his horse and never woke up."

"Oh, geez. Where is his body?"

"Don't worry, I took care of all that. But you need to take care of the horse. I can't do it anymore."

"There is a horse?" This part did not seem like winning the lottery. "Where is it?"

"It's in the barn behind the old house you're about to inherit. Just a few days ago, I left her with plenty of water, hay, and some grain. But she'll run out any day now. You'll want to get one of those rakes to clean up the stall, if you know what I mean. The shovel that's there doesn't cut it."

My head throbbed from the overload of information and sudden responsibility. I blew out a breath and stood ready to take the keys Buck held so tightly. "Come on, man, I've got things to do."

"There's one more requirement. The good news is that you will be able to handle both requirements at the same time."

Now I was scratching my head as I sat back down, exhausted.

"It will be fun. You must turn that big old house into a haunted house and open it up to the community on Halloween. It needs to be a good one and have a minimum of 100 visitors that night. Your uncle was not your average man. I think the word I'm looking for is eccentric."

What was my uncle—an uncle I didn't know existed — thinking? He didn't know me, or maybe he did. Still, why would he care about that big old house now? He was dead.

"A courier will come by on November 1 with the deed to the property and permanent set of keys."

"What are the keys in your hand for?"

"These are keys to the lockbox on the front door. The keys inside that box will open the temporary lock installed about a month before your uncle passed."

Buck handed over the lockbox keys, and I hurried outside in desperate need of fresh air.

Buck shouted after me, "There is a really cool Halloween store set up just a block from the airport. You might want to pick up a few things."

Autumn

The hum of the large jet's engines and the murmur of voices lulled me into a light sleep. My peaceful dozing ended abruptly when I heard the captain announce over the plane's speakers that we'd be making an unscheduled stop.

With all the flights I had under my belt, I'd never experienced an unscheduled stop. I turned to the passenger sitting next to me and asked, "What's going on? Is someone on board ill?"

"No, dear. It seems the jet itself is the problem. Something mechanical, I think. They said not to worry. But everyone will deplane until the problem is fixed. I hope you brought along a good book to read. I think we are in for a lengthy wait."

My concerns faded slightly. "As a matter of fact, I did." Along with my fancy new camera, I had two books in my bag: The pumpkin and spice novel for book club and a New Hampshire travel guide. "I'm afraid I dozed off for a bit. Do we know where this temporary—"

SLAM! Boom! The landing, so sudden and shocking, caused some of the passengers to scream, and now the large jet screeched down the runway with its wings rocking. It swerved sideways before coming to a stop.

I looked out the window and saw several fire trucks with lights flashing and a few buses driving toward us. Thank goodness for that because the terminal was a ways off.

Over the speaker, a flight attendant spoke with urgency. "Please take all of your items with you. You will not be returning to this plane."

One passenger toward the back of the jet said loudly, "Looks like the plane has a fuel leak."

The atmosphere inside the jet immediately became chaotic as people hurried to open the overhead bins, gather their belongings, and push their way to the front. Others dashed for the closest door, leaving their things behind.

Though an experienced flyer, this event was all new to me. I began to sweat, and my body trembled. Had I created bad karma for myself? I hadn't been truthful with my mother. No, I flat-out lied. Maybe I deserved this delay in my vacation and the anxious feeling that rumbled inside me.

"Dear, do you have all your things?" my seatmate asked.

I nodded.

"Then stand right in front of me. I won't let anyone knock you down. People are overreacting. If we were in immediate danger, the emergency doors would open, and we'd be slipping down a big slide."

"Thanks for the information and for playing both the guard and tackle positions."

The woman laughed. "You know football?"

"Sure do. Spent many hours sitting next to my father watching football games on Sunday. That was the only thing he'd stop work for."

Between wading through the unruly crowd and boarding the bus, it took more than thirty minutes before I stood inside the terminal gazing up at the list of departures on one of the airport screens. I soon learned that I was in Connecticut at the Tweed-New Haven Regional Airport and that there were no flights going to Boston until tomorrow. I would miss the connecting flight that would have taken me to the Lebanon Municipal Airport.

"Attention passengers arriving via flight 5261, please proceed to Gate 7."

The announcer repeated that message several times over the loudspeaker. I hurried to that gate and got in line behind other passengers from my flight. All the airline was able to offer was various types of ground transportation. None of those options would get me to Boston in time to catch my next flight, and very few flights flew from Boston to Lebanon, so I was destined to miss almost two days of my 10-day fall vacation. And I was looking at spending a sleepless night in the airport. *Yes. Definitely bad karma at work.*

I requested to have my luggage brought to me rather than be sent ahead without me. I stayed close to Gate 7 until my large suitcase arrived. After that, to pass the time, I walked all over the airport, pulling that big, rolling bag up and down different aisles, passing gates— I counted fourteen—and glancing often at the arrivals/departures screens hoping an earlier flight to Boston would miraculously pop up. Maybe I should have taken them up on a bus ride to Boston. Too late now.

When I came to a moving walkway, I decided to try that for a change of pace, although this was the first time I'd been on one while in charge of my luggage. I surprised myself by inventing an easier method for traveling along the moving walkway. A simple adjustment. Instead of pulling the large suitcase behind me, I pushed it ahead of me. Proud of myself and managing quite well, it wasn't long before I declared that traveling alone wasn't so bad.

Picking up the pace of my steps brought on a giggle. "It feels like I'm flying through the airport."

From somewhere in the bottom of my cross-body bag, I heard my phone chime. As I fumbled to retrieve it, a wave of panic flooded my thinking. What if it was my mother or worse, my father?

At last, the phone was in my hand, and I saw the caller was Allison.

"Hello?"

"Hi, Autumn. Just checking in. Has the limo picked you up in Lebanon yet?"

"Afraid not. I didn't even make it to Boston. The plane had mechanical problems, and we landed somewhere in Connecticut."

"You sound a little out of breath. Are you all right?"

"Yeah. I'm walking on one of those moving walkways pushing my suitcase ahead of me, and—"

I yelped. The movement below my feet suddenly

stopped, but I didn't. My body propelled forward, causing me to trip over my suitcase. The phone went flying, and I lay sprawled on the airport floor. I'd realized the moving walkway had come to an end a little too late. Now, even the words inside my head felt shaky.

"Ma'am. Can I give you a hand?"

I looked up expecting an airport employee, but instead, there stood the most handsome man I'd ever laid eyes on, wearing hiking boots and jeans.

"I'm not sure I can get up quite yet," I said, my voice shaking, my body trembling.

"Okay then. I'll join you on the floor, but first, let's scoot you and your bag a few feet from the walkway. Wouldn't want another traveler to trip over us."

No doubt about it, I must have hit my head, and this was just a dream or maybe a concussion. Meetings like this don't happen in real life. Maybe this wasn't real life. What if the malfunctioning plane had crashed? That would mean—Oh, no. No, no!

"My name is Ranger. What's yours?"

"Autumn. I flew in from Cape Coral, Florida, but wasn't supposed to land here. The plane had some trouble."

"Yeah, I heard about that. So your destination was Boston?"

I relayed a condensed version of my day and then remembered my phone and Allison. "I've got to find my phone. I was talking to my friend when I tripped, and the phone took off on its own. I'm sure she's worried sick."

Ranger took his phone from his back pocket, pressed a few numbers, and said, "We lost a cell phone just a few minutes ago near Gate 14. Anyone turn it in?" All was silent for a few moments. "Okay, thanks."

He sounded happy. I waited with hopeful anticipation. "Someone turned it in already?"

He nodded. "Let's go get it. It's only a gate away. While we walk, you can tell me more about your destination." He tilted his head in the direction we needed to go and nodded. We both reached for the suitcase handle and both hands arrived there at the exact same moment. Ranger patted my hand. "Let me help you with this. It's almost bigger than you."

I tried to hide my overreaction to his mere touch, hoping he hadn't noticed. We began walking slowly toward the next gate. It took me a moment to regain my composure before I said, "After landing in Boston, I was to catch the connecting flight that would take me to Lebanon, New Hampshire."

A smile formed on his face. "That is an amazing coincidence."

"It is?" I asked. "I don't understand."

His smile—warm, friendly—charmed me. Of course, I'd been charmed by characters in romance novels, but never by a real live man.

"I'm headed to New Hampshire too."

"There aren't any more flights going to Boston or

New Hampshire today. I checked." I spoke with authority.

"There's one." He took my hand and led me toward a nearby window. "See that blue and white plane straight ahead?"

"I do. That little plane is flying to Lebanon?" I couldn't help but laugh. "I don't think my suitcase will fit inside." What did he have in mind? Perhaps he was teasing.

"It will fit in the storage compartment. The backseat would normally hold two average-size passengers, but not today. There is room for you up front."

"How do you know all this?"

He shrugged and said, "It's my plane, and I'm the pilot."

I looked at the plane, then at Ranger. "Why would you take me to New Hampshire?"

"I don't know. I usually like to fly alone, but you need a ride, and it feels right."

It did feel right, and that admission frightened me more than flying in a tiny plane with a stranger. I attempted to stir up some intelligent reasons to reject his offer. None came.

"Let's get my phone. After I call Allison back, I'll be ready for takeoff," I said, literally throwing my usual caution to the wind. "Since I'll be the only person flying with you this trip, does that make me the co-pilot?"

"Hmm. Not on this trip. Today, you're one of my passengers."

One of his passengers? I shrugged as we approached the gate where my phone had been turned in. I showed my ID and then the agent handed over the phone. I quickly scrolled to Allison's contact and pressed the Call icon.

"What the hell happened to you?" she said, exasperated.

"Hello to you too. I'm okay. Just took a little fall and my phone went flying. I wanted you to know that I'm fine." Then, I whispered, "Better than fine."

"What's that supposed to mean?"

"There is too much to explain right now. Got to go. My pilot wants to arrive before sunset."

"Call me later when you get settled. We may need to revamp your escape plan. Your mother knows we're not together."

Chapter Four

Ranger

I helped Autumn adjust her seat belt and headphones before walking to the other side of my plane and settling into my seat. "I'm going to be busy for a few minutes, so sit back and relax."

The woman seemed on edge ever since she spoke with her girlfriend. I wondered if she regretted flying off with a stranger. That would make total sense. Or maybe it was the small plane. Some folks won't even sit in a plane like this. Either way, I'd find out for sure in a while. I now had work to do, and, with this special cargo, I'd be extra cautious as I went through all the pre-takeoff protocol.

"Position and hold," I heard the controller say through my headphones.

"Roger-wilco," I replied.

"Cleared for takeoff."

"Roger."

Once we were away from the tower and no more communications were expected, I knew I could enjoy flying my plane home with this pretty, petite woman with long, dark red hair on board.

"You weren't kidding about your backseat being full. What's with the sheets covering your cargo? It looks like you're transporting ghosts," Autumn said as she gave my arm a soft punch.

"Funny you should say that because, in a way, I am."

I noticed a frown combined with a questioning look spread across her face. I wanted the topic of ghosts and the occupants of the back seat to disappear. However, I didn't possess that kind of talent. As I thought about how to tell her what I was carrying, she reached around and took a peek under one of the sheets.

She quickly gasped, and then I heard a giggle.

Glancing over my shoulder, I concluded that her ring or bracelet must have caught a frayed edge of the sheet, causing it to fall off and expose a life-size witch, warts and all. It all happened so fast.

"Aw, geez," I said, wiping the newly formed sweat from my brow. I could not share in the fun. So much for pretending my cargo did not exist.

"Are you able to throw the fallen sheet back over the witch? ASAP? I'd really appreciate that."

"I'll try." She tried unsuccessfully three times before she unfastened her seat belt and began moving toward the back. She glanced at me. "Is that okay? It will only take me a second if I'm closer and use both hands."

"Sure, but hurry."

Just as the ghost, the werewolf, and most of the witch were hidden once again from my view, I had to direct the plane to make a sharp dip to the right, causing Autumn to lose what precarious balance she had. She fell to the left, taking the two remaining sheets with her.

"I'm so sorry," I said. "A flock of birds was right in front of us, and I had to bypass them quickly. Are you okay?"

She didn't answer right away, which worried me. "Autumn, talk to me."

"I'll be all right. My knee is a little sore, and my head is in a vampire's lap, or maybe it's a werewolf. I'm not sure. I just know there's blood on its mouth."

I didn't dare turn around but reached my arm back toward her. "Take my hand, so I can help you up. Then sit back down in your seat as fast as you can. It's going to get bumpy for a while. Buckle up."

Just knowing that a ghost, a werewolf, and a partially covered witch were staring at the back of my head gave me the chills and the creeps, and it brought back a horrific memory as if it were yesterday.

Martin

"Martin, it seems our fantasy vacation winner never made it to Boston. Some kind of plane trouble."

"How do you know that?" Martin asked.

"I check on everything I'm able to. You do the rest. That is how we've always operated. All it took was a few clever phone calls and a lie or two to get the information I wanted."

"So, we're good for now?"

"No, this simple, one-person fantasy vacation has gotten off to a difficult start. Today's problem is that no one knows where Autumn went after the unscheduled landing at the Tweed-New Haven Airport."

"I'll find her, without her knowledge, and get her headed in the right direction."

"Thank you, Martin. I can always count on you."

Ranger

Finally, the turbulence subsided, the back seat creatures stayed put, and, the best part, Autumn wasn't mad. In fact, she wanted to pay me for flying her to the Lebanon Municipal Airport. Of course, I turned down her offer.

"I was going fly right by there anyway. So hang on to your money."

"Does that mean you were not planning to land there?"

"That's right, before I met you, I was going to land at one of the Forest Service's small air fields, but it's okay. I can fuel up while you are . . . what does happen next for you?"

"A limo will pick me up there and take me to the Sugar Lane Inn. Then tomorrow, I will begin doing a few touristy things and take some award-winning photographs of all the glorious fall color New Hampshire has to offer. I'm creating a portfolio that I'll use when I apply for graduate studies in photojournalism."

"I have a great view of fall colors right now," I said. "Autumn colors, to be more specific." I paused and waited for a reaction. When none came, I went a little further with my teasing. "Shouldn't you have a few freckles to go with your fall-colored hair?"

She hesitated. "No. I don't have fall-colored hair."

I hesitated, unsure how to take her comment. Her hair was red with some gold and did resemble fall colors. My cleverness went unnoticed, so I moved on and offered to take her flying some other day for some aerial photography.

"That would be wonderful. How can I ever repay you for your kindness?"

"As a matter of fact, there is something you could help me with. Want to hear about that?"

"Of course, I'm happy to—"

The radio squawked. The static made it difficult to understand the words, but I got the gist. Bad news. The Lebanon Municipal Airport was closed due to a freak, early snowstorm.

"What do we do?" Autumn asked with a bit of panic in her voice.

"There's only one choice now. Unfortunately, you

won't make it to the Sugar Lane Inn tonight. Your accommodations will be safe but . . . rustic."

Autumn

It was dusk as we descended toward my new destination for the night, and I saw nothing but trees in every direction.

"Are we landing here? How is that possible?" I asked.

"We're almost there. The runway will come into view in about five minutes."

Sure enough, it did. From the air, it looked more like a wide trail than a runway. Instinctively, I checked to ensure my seat belt was firmly fastened and then clutched my crossbody bag tightly. There was no need for a flight attendant to announce that we were in for a rough landing. Seeing the packed-dirt runway beginning to fill with a thin blanket of snow would suffice.

Though focused on piloting a safe landing, Ranger appeared calm and cool while I braced for the imminent touchdown. First came a thud and then a bit of bouncing before we were fully on the ground. All in all, the landing was far smoother than most of the large jet landings I'd experienced.

"Impressive," I said. The moment the plane came to a complete stop and Ranger cut the engine, I had to ask, "Where am I?"

"We are in the White Mountain National Forest.

We got lucky. Not as much snow here, at least not yet. Stay put for a few minutes. I will drive my truck closer to the plane and warm it up before you get in."

"Okay, thanks."

This man was so nice and considerate. But I wondered if he might be too nice, too good to be true. I'd heard on the news and seen a few movies in which men appearing to be friendly were actually abducting innocent women and intended to inflict great bodily harm, even death.

With that horrific thought on my mind, I jerked when Ranger opened the passenger door of the plane. He helped me down and then into his truck.

"Where to now?"

"To my cabin. It's not a five-star hotel, but it will keep us warm and dry for the night. It's only a few minutes from here."

My heart was good with that answer, but my rational mind? Not so much. For a split second, I wished my father were here. I'd wanted independence and to be able to travel alone for once. I hadn't wished to be alone in the middle of a huge forest in a storm with a stranger.

Night had finally fallen as we drove away from the airfield. The truck's headlights were the only illumination until the weak glow of Ranger's porch light came into view.

Ranger parked in front of the cabin and then turned

to me and asked, "Would you like me to bring your suit-case inside the cabin?"

"Yes, please," I said while my heart and mind were still dueling. I rooted for my heart to be the winner, but my mind wasn't willing to back down just yet.

Ranger lifted the suitcase from the truck and hurried in ahead of me to turn on some lights. The cabin was cozy, and soon after he lit a fire in the fireplace, the temperature was tolerable.

"You want a beer? Beer and water are the only drinks I've got right now. I don't get to spend much time here."

I surprised myself and agreed to have a beer. Perhaps it was just what I needed to take the annoying, unhelpful edge off.

We sat on the sofa sipping our drinks and watching the fire as it crackled and popped and gave off a delicious pine scent.

"Why do you live way out here in the woods?"

"This is where I work. I'm a forest ranger, often up in the air assisting with wildlife management or fire control. I'm allowed to keep my personal plane with the forest service's planes and equipment."

"So . . . you're Ranger the ranger?"

He nodded and grinned. "Yep. My parents had no idea that I'd be a ranger someday. It seemed to work okay for quite a while. My official nameplate says Ranger Lee. Hey, you want a tour of your accommoda-tion? It will be quick."

He showed me around, pointing out the obvious. The living area and the kitchen were all one room. There was one small bedroom containing a double bed, a chest of drawers, and a small closet with a door made of fabric. "There is a tiny bathroom out back," he said.

"Wait. The bathroom is outside?"

Ranger laughed. "The original outhouse is still there and functional, but let me show you your other option."

I sighed, greatly relieved seeing the tiny indoor bathroom I'd mistaken for a kitchen closet door just moments ago.

"All I've got in the way of food is a small variety of canned goods and several frozen TV dinners. I could pop two of them into the microwave. We should cook those right away, just in case the power goes out due to the storm."

"TV dinners? I don't think I've ever eaten one." I stifled a giggle. "I've had steak dinners and seafood dinners. To my knowledge, TVs are not edible. And you don't even have a TV."

Ranger appeared to be thinking. "If I did have a TV, we'd be watching it while we ate." He sounded so matter-of-fact.

"Since you don't have a TV, can I assume that to be perfectly correct, we'll be eating fireplace dinners?"

"Don't tell me you're a perfectionist. Tell me you're kidding."

I stood and slowly walked around the room, meticulously straightening anything that seemed crooked or out of place. From the corner of my eye, I saw him watching me intently and frowning.

"Oh, all right. I am kidding, but I've never eaten a TV dinner in my entire life. And that is the truth." I could not recall feeling so playful ever before, and I loved it, despite a malfunctioning jet, a snowstorm, and my fantasy vacation going sideways. What would tomorrow bring?

"What about a microwave dinner? Everybody eats those once in a while." Ranger seemed confident with that statement.

I shook my head. "Not in my family. We've always had a live-in cook and also a housekeeper."

His frown returned. "So, you're a spoiled little rich girl? You must hate being here in this funky old cabin with no room service, no Jacuzzi, no real heat. For tonight, all you have is me—one tired, poorly paid forest ranger."

He stepped into the kitchen area, grabbed two boxes from the freezer, opened them, and then placed them into the microwave before twisting off the top of another beer for himself. I felt awful. Was I a spoiled little rich girl? I hadn't meant to hurt his feelings, but that was exactly what I'd done.

I'd had little experience with men except for my father. He was strict, strong, fearless, and very wealthy. Sometimes, I thought he was an unnatural superhero without human emotions. Nothing seemed to faze him. Would I see a different side of Father when he learned about my fantasy vacation and venturing far away from home alone? Whenever I hinted at rebelling, Mother reminded me that Father's name was William, and *vehement protector* was the original meaning of his name. Apparently, he took his name's origin a bit too seriously.

Ranger pulled a small, low table over to the sofa where I sat, and then he went back to the microwave to retrieve the hot dinners.

"Do you want turkey or meatloaf?" he asked.

"Turkey, please."

Our eyes met as he bent down to set the dinners on the table, and we both spoke at once. "I'm sorry."

"You have nothing to be sorry for," he said. "I'm the jerk here. I lashed out at you for your fortunate home life, something you had no control over. Will you accept my apology?"

"Of course I will."

"Why did you say you were sorry?" he asked. "You had done nothing wrong."

"I hurt your feelings."

He paused and after a moment said, "That's my problem, not yours. I should be tougher and—"

"No, you're just right. The food smells delicious. Let's eat."

And so we did.

Ranger

I came out of the bedroom carrying sheets, blankets, and a pillow.

"You don't need to sleep on the sofa for me," said Autumn. "This is your place, and you've already gone above and beyond."

I took advantage of the opportunity to add some humor. "You're the one sleeping on the couch tonight." The look of surprise on her face made me grin.

"Sure, of course," she stammered. "That's more than fair."

"Want to know why?"

"Only if you want to tell me."

"The only heat available comes from the fireplace. You will be much warmer here than in the bedroom. I only request that you're okay with me keeping my door open so that a little of the heat finds its way back to me."

Autumn nodded and smiled. I had to admit that I loved her smile and her gentle ways. The women I worked with were tough; they had to be. And although I liked those skillful, talented women, I was never inclined to hook up with any of them. Just as well. Women were complicated.

"I've got a busy day tomorrow, so we're going have to get up before the sun. I'll drive you to the Sugar Lane Inn first thing, and you can get on with your photo-taking vacation. Then, I have to go see a horse."

"How can I ever thank you?" Autumn asked as she turned my old couch into a small, narrow bed.

An idea popped up. "You know, a personal task is

coming up soon, and I could use some help with it. I'll catch up with you in a day or two after you're all settled in and know your itinerary."

"You'd better give me a hint, or I'll never get to sleep."

"Okay, if you insist. The task involves a haunted house."

Autumn pulled the covers back and then slid between them, leaving only her eyes exposed. She looked directly at me.

I winked and went to bed.

Chapter Five

Autumn

The room was dark except for a faint orange glow coming from a few remaining coals in the fireplace. "Ranger. Ranger? Is it time to get up?" I said softly.

When no answer came, I wrapped up in one of the blankets from the sofa and tiptoed over to the open door of his bedroom. A small bedside lamp illuminated the room just enough for me to see that Ranger was not there. When I called out louder, there was still no reply. He must be outside.

I had slept in my clothes; something else I'd never done before. I added several more layers to stay warm as I prepared to head outside. Opening the front door, I saw no sign of the sun, but dawn had definitely arrived, blanketing the surrounding area in a soft gray. Stepping out, I nearly tripped over something, but what? It wasn't very big—probably just a large stray cat—and it dashed away quickly. It also took my breath away for a few frightening seconds.

Breathing normally now and glancing around, a sudden, additional fright hit me. Ranger's truck was gone. *Don't panic!* Just because I was alone in the middle of a huge forest and the missing ranger was the only person on the planet who knew where I was, was no reason to overreact. Like hell, it wasn't. I dashed back inside to see if he had left me a note.

If there were a note, I couldn't find it. Neither could I merely sit there and do nothing. The cabin's temperature was already chilly because of the dying fire, so I grabbed two logs from the porch and added them to the fire, hoping I'd placed them correctly. One more thing I'd never done before. Three firsts in less than twelve hours.

Last night, Ranger said that we'd need to leave early and also something about a horse. Had he left without me? All sorts of reasons for his absence came to mind. The most logical one involved the horse. Perhaps he chose to handle that task before driving me to the Sugar Lane Inn. Yeah. I'll go with that theory.

Almost an hour had passed with no sign of Ranger, or anyone for that matter. But the sunshine now streaming in the window gave me the courage to explore outside. I decided to take my camera, shoot some photos, and stay close to the cabin. Surely, he'd be back soon.

There were no beautifully colored, deciduous trees within sight, so I photographed the cabin and a few pine trees. Not many trees like these in Cape Coral. Then I saw it. It was likely the animal that had been lying in front of the door when I stepped out earlier. The furry red fox was the perfect adorable subject. I focused so intently that I failed to notice Ranger driving up.

"I tried to call you, but there was no answer. Are you all right?"

I pulled out my cell phone to check the screen. "It seems I turned the ringer off during the night and forgot to turn it back on. Sorry. But I put another log on the fire and took some photos while waiting for you."

"All's well then, now that I know you're okay. I brought donuts."

"You must have gotten up very early. Did you go see the horse?"

"Nope. Had to get a co-worker out of a jam," he said, shaking his head. "She can climb a tree, swing an ax, and wrestle a fire hose better than most men, but this morning, she couldn't change a tire."

That situation did seem odd, and Ranger seemed annoyed. It was none of my business, so I let it go.

"Let's eat donuts while you show me some of your photographic work. We do need to get going in about twenty minutes. We'll stop for coffee on the way."

The donuts hit the spot. I multi-tasked, showing Ranger a few of my photos and getting my things ready to go while stuffing my mouth with the best chocolate donut I'd ever eaten.

"These are great photos of Red. Would you mind sending a couple of them to my phone later?"

"You have a pet fox named Red?"

"No. She's a wild animal. I'd never try to tame it or even feed it. It does seem to like it around here, though."

"Yes. It seems that way. I nearly tripped over Red this morning. She was laying right at your front door."

We headed out toward the truck. I saw Red sitting at the tree line, and I felt my cheeks lift at the sight of her. I also saw the three sheet-covered ghouls seated in the truck. I guess they were coming along for the ride.

Ranger

"Ranger, do you know how long will it take to get to the Sugar Lane Inn?" Autumn asked, looking at me with those soft, tawny brown eyes.

"If the weather and the road conditions are kind to us, about forty-five minutes."

"I take it you've been there before."

How should I answer her question? With the truth? Did it even matter? We were just two people passing in the night. I helped her with a ride north in my plane, and she would help me transform a house, soon to be mine, into a haunted house. She was still looking at me, waiting for my answer.

"I did stay there a few times years ago . . . trying to

impress a lady friend. But I'd know the Inn's location without having had that experience. New Hampshire is a small state, and I've flown over almost every inch of it. How's that for an answer?"

"It will do for now," Autumn said with a somewhat teasing tone. "Did you impress her?"

"It didn't take long to figure out that she was more impressed with my plane than with me. That was the end of our brief encounter."

"Well, I'm impressed with you. You're a handsome, kind man who loves nature and animals. What more could a girl ask for? Oh, yeah. A plane." She giggled.

We didn't talk for the remainder of the drive. We sat in comfortable silence. At least I did. Guess I shouldn't speak for her.

I pulled up to the Inn's entrance to unload Autumn's luggage but was quickly waved over to a small, nearby parking area. I found an empty spot and parked. Quickly, a security guard approached us and asked to see my ID and then Autumn's.

Autumn and I made eye contact and shrugged. "What's going on? Is there a problem?" I asked the guard.

He didn't answer but turned away and spoke into a radio attached to his shoulder. "She's here. The missing woman is here."

A large, strong-looking man walked toward my truck and then stood next to my window. "I'll take it from here," he said to me. Then he leaned down and looked across the cab at Autumn. "It's good to meet you, Ms. Reed. We worried when you did not arrive on schedule."

Who was this guy? The manager? He was acting more like a cop. I could see a flicker of fear in Autumn's eyes, so I stepped up, not knowing what the heck was going on. I'd get to the bottom of this. Autumn and I got out of the truck and walked around to the back. I lifted the large piece of luggage out and then took Autumn's hand. She offered it willingly.

"I'll take it from here," I said sternly.

We walked to the front of the Inn, and I stayed by Autumn's side as she checked in. The desk clerk was friendly and helpful. The stranger kept his distance as well as an eye on both of us.

"Will you be all right?" I asked her after she completed her check in. "I hate to leave you here. This feels odd, to say the least. But I need to go meet this horse that has been somewhat abandoned and left in my care."

"Go. I'll be fine. And, thank you for everything."

She stood up on her toes and kissed my cheek.

"I will be back in a couple of hours. I'd like to talk to you. Or I will be the one acting like a cop." I brushed her cheek with the back of my hand and headed out.

Autumn

"Well, Miss Autumn Reed, you gave us quite a scare."

Seriously, who was this guy? I gave him an annoyed smirk. Right now, I wanted nothing more than to see my room and unpack. Waving to the desk clerk and pointing at my luggage, a sturdy woman arrived, loaded everything but my purse onto a cart, and we began walking. The stranger tagging along.

"I did the best I could after my plane landed unexpectedly in the wrong place. Without the help of the ranger you saw me with, I might still be in New Haven or, at best, Boston."

"In that case, I'd have found you yesterday. What makes you think that man is a ranger? He wasn't wearing the uniform."

"Oh, he's a ranger, all right. A forest ranger and pilot for the White Mountain National Forest Service."

"You will need to stay close to the Inn for at least an hour," the man stated.

"And why is that?" I was exasperated. I didn't even know his name or what his job was here at the Inn.

"Some local law enforcement may wish to ask you a few questions."

"Why the questions? I've done nothing wrong. And who are you?"

He reached out his hand and said, "My name is Martin. I work with The Fantasy Maker, and you were a missing person for almost 24 hours."

He handed me a business card and walked away.

Not much info on that card, merely his first name and a phone number. It would have been nice to have that yesterday. I decided that if someone showed up within the hour, I'd ask a few questions of my own. If not, I would walk the beautiful grounds here at the Sugar Lane Inn and snap my first colorful fall photos.

Ranger

I added the address of my future property to the maps app on my phone before leaving the parking lot of the Sugar Lane Inn. It was a twenty-minute drive from here. That was convenient. As I pulled out of the parking lot, I turned up the radio. My fingers tapped to the beat and I began to sing along with Garth Brooks and his song "Friends in Low Places." I felt a smile take control of my face. And then I remembered, I don't sing. I can play the guitar, but I don't sing.

The cause of this phenomenon was three-fold. The sun was shining brightly now, I was heading to my new-to-me large old house with a horse (I'd wanted a dog someday, not a horse), and maybe a relationship with Autumn—the woman, not the season—was emerging.

As I drove along the country roads, I noticed a feed store and decided to stop in for horse food since Buck had let me know the horse was almost out.

Walking into the store, I knew I was out of my element. I waved at a young man who clearly worked there and asked him for help.

"I need some food for a horse," I said.

"Just one horse?" he asked.

"I think so. I hope so."

"What kind of horse and how old is it?"

"I have no idea. Just round up enough basic food and treats to last a week until I know more about this horse. Horses do like treats, right?"

The young man chuckled and then signaled for me to follow him.

Ah, the country life. A far cry from living deep within a forest. It didn't take long to fill up the bed of my truck with a bale of hay, some alfalfa, and a bag of apple-flavored treats. The young man threw in a strange-looking rake and a book about caring for horses at no charge. Guess he figured out I was a rookie.

I got back on the road and it wasn't long before I heard the automated voice on my phone tell me I had arrived at my destination.

A four-foot-high rock wall marked the property line. After opening the screeching gate—I'd apply some WD40 on the way out—I pulled in and drove down the long driveway. There it stood, larger than I expected, and, in my estimation, it already resembled a haunted house.

Hearing the horse neigh, I got down to follow the sound and, hopefully, locate the barn. Nothing that looked like a barn stood within the rock wall boundary. But the horse continued to call out, sounding more and more frantic with each passing moment.

A good distance from the house stood the only other structure on the property. It wasn't a barn by any stretch of one's imagination. It might have been a place to store vehicles in the past, but it definitely wasn't meant for a horse. But that's where the whinnying was coming from. The horse must be inside. At about thirty paces from the double doors, I called out to the animal.

"Hey, buddy. I'm here. You're going to be okay."

At the sound of my voice, the horse kicked the doors open and bounded out wildly. I wasn't prepared for that and didn't know if it was glad to be out, happy to see a human, or mad as hell about being left alone for so long. It kicked and bucked before coming to a sudden, screeching halt just three feet in front of me.

Neither of us moved, and I wondered how long this stand-off would last. Having no experience with horses, I deferred to the animal and let it make the first move. What seemed like an eternity was probably just a few minutes. The horse took a step closer, walked past me, turned around, came back, and stood at my side.

That felt okay, even good. I walked toward the building where the horse had been locked up and the animal followed, but he didn't want to go in. I soon knew why. The interior was dark, damp, and wreaked of death, and who knows what else.

I walked back to my truck and then drove it down closer to the broken double doors. I grabbed the bandana I'd been keeping in my toolbox and secured it around my face to minimize the smell.

Although I had a long day ahead of me doing things that didn't involve a horse, I needed to take care of this first.

I gave the horse a few treats and then braved the inside of the building. I dragged a metal container out into the fresh air assuming this was or could be the horse's water dish, and began my search for a hose and a water source.

I did find a lengthy though somewhat cracked hose, but no water spigot. Oh, well. No time like the present to look inside the house. My temporary keys worked, and my bandana continued to serve me well inside. Not that the place smelled of death, but it wreaked of mold, dust, and stale air.

Fortunately, the water in the house worked, and I could hook the hose to the kitchen faucet and drag it outside, though it didn't reach the metal container. Was I stuck in a one-step-forward-and-two-steps-back kind of day?

The horse waited patiently by the kitchen window. For the next two hours, it followed me around like a puppy. *I always wanted a dog but not one this large.* The horse was growing on me, though. I felt so sorry for its recent experience, and who knows what happened before that.

I had lost track of time, and when I finally sat down for a break, I checked the clock and realized I was late. I had told Autumn I'd be back in two hours but I couldn't leave the horse quite yet. While the water filled the container, I scattered several piles of hay around the house's exterior.

I decided to call the Inn. Autumn was in her suite and easy to connect with. For once, I lucked out.

"Hi, sweetie. I, I mean Autumn. Everything is a little strange here. The horse has had a rough time of it. The good news? The property is not far from the Inn."

"Great! Come and get me."

"Really? Do you think your keepers there will let you leave? Is that big guy still lurking around?"

"I haven't seen him in a while, but I'm an adult. Just because I've been awarded this unique vacation here in New Hampshire doesn't give anyone the right to control my life. Come get me."

"Are you sure? It's kind of disgusting and dirty. Do you have any old clothes? No, of course, you don't. I withdraw the question. At least bring warm clothes with you. I don't know if there is heat or a fireplace or—"

"None of that matters. Hurry! I'll be watching for you."

"I'm on my way."

I hoped this horse wasn't a jumper. I wanted her to be there when I got back.

Chapter Six

Autumn

Mirror, mirror on the wall, don't want to see myself at all. Covering that mirror was the first thing I'd done upon my arrival at the Inn. I'd requested an extra bed sheet and some duct tape. It wasn't pretty, but it would do. Would the housekeeping staff think I'm crazy? Would dreadful rumors about me circulate throughout this beautiful establishment? Probably. Still, that was better than keeping my eyes closed whenever I was in my suite's bedroom.

No time to deal with that now. Ranger would be here soon, and I had two things to do before his arrival. I multitasked like never before. First, I downloaded a book to my iPad about caring for horses as I walked toward the Inn's gift shop. I'd seen several racks of clothing earlier. I crossed my fingers, hoping to find a pair of jeans.

I found dozens of fancy jeans with sequins, embroidery, and lots of holes and slits, and all were low cut.

"Do you have any regular jeans, you know, plain jeans?" I asked the clerk.

"I do have some in the back. What size, dear?"

"Hmm. In slacks and dresses, I usually wear a size 6, though most of my clothing is altered to fit me." The woman looked me up and down.

"I'll bring out three pair. A size 4, a size 6, and a size 8."

I glanced around the shop at the jewelry, knick-knacks, and cards as I waited for the clerk to return. She smiled at me as she emerged from a back room carrying three pair of jeans. She handed them to me, and I gave her my suite number, saying I'd bring back the ones that did not fit.

"Take your time, dear. No one else here will want to purchase those jeans today."

"Thanks."

I hustled back to my suite, hoping I'd have time to try on the jeans before Ranger arrived. I could hear my room phone ringing as I swiped the key card in the door's handle. I ran inside and grabbed the phone just in time.

"Hello?" I said breathlessly.

"Are you all right?"

It was Ranger.

"Absolutely. I've been rushing around. No big deal. Are you here?"

"Yes. Do you want me to come to your suite?"

No, I did not want him here in my room. He might see my hanging sheet. No, neither of us was ready for that revelation.

"I'll meet you in the lobby in a few minutes. I have to take care of something first."

"Okay, take your time," he said.

I hung up and quickly tried on all the jeans. The size 6 fit well enough for going to visit a horse. My parents would cringe if they saw me right now. I laughed at the possibility, then dashed out the door with my bag, my iPad, and my warmest jacket. Ready or not, Ranger, here I come.

The man smiled as I hurried toward him. "All set?" he asked.

I nodded, and the next thing I knew, we were in his truck, which smelled delicious. That was my first joyful shock.

He grinned a boyish grin. "Hamburgers and french fries. I was hungry and thought you might be too."

His thinking was correct. Suddenly starving, I asked, "Does the house where the horse lives have a working microwave?"

"I have no idea. Why do you ask?"

"Just wondered if we'd be able to reheat the burgers when we get there."

"Autumn, we are not waiting another second to

begin eating. If you will pass me a burger and unwrap one for yourself, we can get this show on the road."

"You don't mind if we eat in your truck? Father never allowed us to bring food into our family vehicles."

"Really? I never heard of such a limitation. What's the worst thing that could happen? A few crumbs fall, a drop of ketchup ends up on the steering wheel? Come on now. Eat up before it gets cold."

I unwrapped a burger and handed it to Ranger before unwrapping my own and taking my first savory bite. He smiled at me and then took off out of the parking lot and onto the two-lane road lined with those beautiful trees I couldn't wait to take pictures of.

We arrived at the property's gate just as I took the last bite of my second burger. I couldn't believe I had eaten so much, but I had been absolutely famished and it was the best burger I had had in a long while. I saw the horse right away, standing on the other side of the gate.

"She's beautiful," I said, wadding up the burger wrapper and stuffing it in the bag the food had come in. I'd seen racehorses from a private box a few times but never one up close.

"Are you a horse owner?" Ranger asked.

I laughed and shook my head. "Our family isn't into animals, especially not big ones. Even so, I was one of those little girls who thought having a pony sounded like fun. Oh, well. I'll live vicariously now while I'm here with your horse."

"Let's not call this horse my horse just yet," he said, stepping out of the truck and walking toward the gate. The horse shook its head up and down and from side to side as he opened the gate. Then she pranced around Ranger, stopping to nudge her nose against his back.

This horse that wasn't his seemed very happy to see him.

Ranger was back in the truck in no time. He drove slowly through the opening, not wanting to upset the horse in any way. As soon as we cleared the gate, I started to jump out to close and latch it. Ranger grabbed my arm and opened his mouth to say something, but I cut him off.

"I've got this," I assured him.

He released me with a smile that he was still holding when I returned to the truck.

The horse led the way to the building that Ranger called the barn. Once inside, I saw that it was more like a car collector's giant garage, though it was dark, dingy, old, and musty. The horse remained outside as Ranger showed me around. My heart broke for this poor animal having to live in such conditions.

"What's the plan?" I asked.

"Still thinking about that. I need to make a section of this building more livable for the horse." Ranger threw a pile of hay outside not too far from the door where the horse could eat and keep an eye on us at the same time. That pleased all three of us.

There was so much rusty, cobweb-covered unidentified junk in every direction. I stepped out to be with the horse and took out my phone as well as the business card that guy Martin had given me. He'd told me to call him if I needed anything. I'd test his words right now.

"Miss Autumn, how nice of you to call," Martin answered after the first ring.

"Thank you. How nice of you to answer. I hope you meant what you said because I do need something. It is very important."

"I'm listening."

Without much detail, I gave him the property's address and said I was helping a horse and needed a large dumpster. I bet he had never had a request like mine before. Time would tell if he could make this happen.

I stepped back into the barn and watched Ranger as he continued to move things around. He stood up, looking worn, and then smiled at me.

"Let's go check out the house. Hopefully, it's in better shape than the barn," he announced. "We're calling that building the barn no matter what it was in a previous life."

From the exterior, the house appeared to have three levels, though the top level was very small and likely just an attic.

"It does look like a haunted house," I said with a chuckle. "A real haunted house. It will be perfect after we clean it up and decorate with hay bales, pumpkins, Indian corn, adorable ghosts, maybe a black cat or two."

"Real ones?" His eyes widened, his brows raised.

"We'll see." Was I teasing?

As we walked through the ground floor, I took decorating notes on my cell phone. After flipping several switches, we concluded that the lights did not work or the electricity had been turned off. Ranger hunted down the fuse box while I checked the light bulbs. Out of luck on both counts. Fortunately, enough light streamed in the windows for a cursory look around. Ranger seemed on edge, always looking over his shoulder and at his watch.

Joking, I asked if he had a date.

He frowned but didn't answer.

Now I was the one frowning as we continued our self-guided tour of the first floor of the old house. I expected it to have a dusty, musty scent, but what I didn't expect was a faint flowery scent that occasionally drifted by. Did Ranger smell that too?

An hour later, a loud horn honking attracted our attention and I knew immediately that Martin had come through for me and the dumpster had arrived.

"I'll go open the gate while you select the best location for the large dumpster."

I loved the confused look on Ranger's face when he asked, "That's your doing?"

I nodded.

"Okay, how did you do that?"

"I have magical powers," I said, wiggling my nose.

Ranger

We got right to work on the barn, hauling items we both deemed useless out to the dumpster. We set aside anything that might be someone else's treasure for an estate sale someday. The horse followed our movements, keeping close to us at all times.

"Does the horse have a name?" Autumn asked.

I shrugged, having no answer.

"What about the guy you met in New Haven?"

"His name is Buck Johnson, but I don't think he mentioned any other names. Definitely not the horse's and not even my uncle's name. He didn't have much information to share with me. All he said was, 'Take care of the horse and create a haunted house.'"

"That's what we're doing, right? So what is troubling you?" Autumn asked, looking me straight in the eye.

What was I willing to share with her? The Halloween haunted house project might become difficult for me, and I wasn't convinced I could pull it off. Not fond of failing, second thoughts about this project crept in.

"You should enjoy every day of your vacation here in New Hampshire, taking photos, sightseeing, and whatever is on your scheduled itinerary, and I need to go back to work. I've already missed two days."

I found myself staring at this beautiful, petite young woman with reddish hair who stood there with her hands on her hips, looking very bold and thoughtful, or was she upset with me? I didn't know her well enough to be sure.

"How often does a Forest Service Ranger—you in particular—get called into action after dark?"

Good question. It made me think. "Not often, but I'm on call 24/7. True, the Sugar Lane Inn is not far from this house, but it's a much longer drive to the Forest Service headquarters and my plane."

"I'm here for eight more days. I can get a lot done in that time."

"What's that supposed to mean?"

"It means you can do your forest rangering during the day while I do what I can here, and then we can—"

"No. Absolutely not. I do not want you here alone. That would be foolish, dangerous, and I could not live with myself if anything happened to you."

For some reason, that made her smile.

"I promise I will never be here alone, okay?"

"Who do you have in mind? And the horse doesn't count." That stopped her words from flowing, but she hadn't stopped thinking.

"Hear me out. I have a plan B."

There wasn't much daylight left, which reminded me to call the electric company ASAP, so I suggested we get the horse settled in the much-improved barn, lock up and grab some dinner near the Sugar Lane Inn, where Autumn could explain her plan B before I headed home.

. . .

I agreed to give her new plan a try beginning tomorrow evening. She made it sound simple and workable. I would spend most of the day rangering, as she called it, in the forest while she enjoyed her Fantasy Maker vacation. I'd pick her up around 5 p.m., and we'd spend each evening caring for the horse and cleaning up the first floor of the soon-to-be haunted house.

Only two things bothered me as I drove home alone to my rustic cabin. First, how the hell would I be able to create a haunted house with my childhood Halloween trauma still hanging around? Second, I missed Autumn already.

Chapter Seven

Autumn

Sleep took forever to come, and when it did, it was fitful. Not that I was disturbed by noises from people in the hallway; all was quiet. The commotion in my head was the culprit. My mind swirled with pleasant thoughts of the horse, the house, and Ranger. Even so, occasional visions of the hanging curtain crept in along with the pounding. The pounding?

I shot straight up in bed as I registered that the pounding was coming from the door to the suite.

"Hello?" I said tentatively.

"Miss Autumn, check your room phone," came a voice on the other side of the door. "The desk clerk told me you had several calls come in last night and early this morning."

I scrambled for my clothes. "Martin, is that you?"

"Yes, ma'am," he said from the hallway. "And I've brought your breakfast."

"I'll be right there." I'd never dressed so fast in all my life. Bare-footed and with only slacks and a cream-colored sweater on, I hurried to open the door.

"I'll set the tray on the table by the window," Martin said as he breezed through the door and shuffled past me.

"Thank you." The food smelled delightful, making my stomach rumble.

Anxious to listen to the phone messages in private, I stood ready to move into the bedroom the second he was gone. When he reached for the door handle, I backed slowly through the bedroom door.

He turned and followed me with his eyes. The silence felt awkward, his expression troubling. Finally, he spoke. "Your Jackson tour will leave in exactly one hour. The guide will pick you up from the lobby. Have a great day."

He left as quickly as he showed up. I latched the door behind him and then walked to the suite's phone. I sighed when I saw the flashing red light on the phone, absently tilting my head back in wonder. As I brought my eyes back down to the phone, I saw the sheet I'd hung to hide the huge mirror. Had Martin seen it too? *Push that thought away for now and listen to your messages.* Suddenly, I realized how this morning's situation made no sense. Anyone who knew me would call

78

my cell phone. And why didn't I hear the phone ring? Breakfast would have to wait. I had two mysteries to solve.

I tore the room apart looking for my cell. No luck. It was gone. I called the Inn's operator and asked two questions. Did anyone turn in a cell phone, and why didn't my room's phone ring?

"Sorry about that," the operator said. "Check the bottom of the phone. There should be a small switch there. Just flip it the other way."

"Okay, I did that. What now?"

"Hang up. I'm going to call you."

I hung up and then five seconds later, my phone rang.

"That worked. Thanks. Are the phones usually turned to the no sound position?"

"No, ma'am. Only guests are allowed to do that. I'll check with the housekeeper and see what I can find out."

"Thank you." Next, I pressed the flashing red button, ready to listen.

Message number one: "Hi Autumn. I just want to tell you that I enjoyed our time together today. By the way, I called your cell but got no answer. In case you didn't recognize my voice, this is Ranger. Call me back when you get a minute."

Message number two: Hey Autumn, it's Allison. It's getting difficult here. I feel like I'm caught in the middle of a family feud. Call me!"

Message number three: "It's me again. You're freaking me out. Answer your cell phone, damn it."

I suppose it made sense for Ranger and Allison to be upset. I usually have my cell phone with me and almost always answer it. Then there's the malfunctioning room phone, a weird coincidence for sure. I decided to make some calls just as soon as I finished listening to the remainder of my messages.

Message number four: "Are you all right, darlin'? It's morning, the sun is up, and I still have not heard from you. I'm worried. Where are you? Call me or I'm coming over there."

He called me darlin'. For a brief moment, I felt flushed and hoped I wasn't becoming ill. Perhaps I had a touch of Rangeritis.

Message number five: "Geez, Autumn. Your mom is over at my house talking to my mother about our deceitful plan. I think we are both in big trouble. I don't know what to say, especially since you have disappeared. Should I be angry or scared? Please clarify ASAP."

Five down, one more message to go.

Message number six: "Autumn, this is your mother. I'm worried. Had a nice long talk with Allison and her mother. Even your friend has no idea why no one seems to be able to reach you. I'd gotten used to the idea of your fantasy vacation to take fall photos. I'd even covered for you with your father, but my next call will be to the police if I don't hear from you soon."

Oh, dear. Ranger will have to wait a bit longer. I called Mother right away and explained the trouble with my room's phone, that I'd lost my cell phone, and that everything was wonderful.

"As soon as I find my phone, I'll send you some photos of the Sugar Lane Inn. I'm sorry I wasn't truthful with you and made you worry. Allison planned to come with me, but she backed out at the last minute. I'm not sure why."

"Probably because she came to her senses just in time. From now on, we need to communicate much better so that nothing like this ever happens again. Do you think you can call me every day? Somehow, I will deal with your father. He'll be home in a few days. And he'll be fuming mad for a while. Knowing him, he'll fly up there and force you to come home."

"I really hope not, Mother," I said with a sigh. "I'm having a great time and don't want to leave."

Mother *tsked* on the other end of the line.

"I'll call you tomorrow," I assured her before hanging up.

I wasn't ready to tell her about the man who called me darlin'. I doubted she'd be prepared to hear about him, so I decided to keep Ranger a secret a while longer. After all, we'd only known each other for a couple of days, though I already felt close to him.

At last, I made the call to Ranger, hoping to put an end to his worrying. I let it ring fifteen times. He didn't answer. Had an odd circumstance come up or was this payback?

I called Allison. When she answered, I gave her a truthful explanation for my lack of communication.

"Well, the harm is already done. My parents have forbidden me to see you. In other words, we can't play together anymore."

I giggled for a few seconds.

"I've got to go, Autumn."

Then it dawned on me that she wasn't joking! The line went dead and I sat there looking at my phone in disbelief.

I had displeased my parents, and my best friend wasn't allowed to spend time with me. I wasn't used to being the bad girl, a troublemaker. This was a first, and I did not like the label or how I felt right now. Could this day get any worse?

My dreary thoughts shifted when I heard a knock at the door. Probably housekeeping or room service, but I was in no mood to talk with anyone. Normally, I'd look through the peephole but for some reason threw caution to the wind and opened the door anyway.

"Martin! You're back." I stammered and then suddenly realized I was supposed to meet the tour guide in the lobby.

"And you, Miss Autumn, are late. Come on. This is one of the best fall color locations of your entire vacation. If you hurry, we can catch up with the tour bus."

"It already left?"

He nodded, so I quickly grabbed a piece of toast from the tray, my jacket, and my camera bag. I'd take magnificent fall photos all day long and help Ranger with the haunted house and his horse tonight. Life was good once again.

As we rushed down the hallway, I thought I heard a room phone ringing. Was it coming from my suite? If I went back to check, we'd be too late to catch up with the others. I was looking forward to capturing award-winning photos during this excursion to Jackson and its surrounding landscape, so I chose to keep up with Martin.

Martin and I were able to catch up with the tour group and as I joined them, I bid Martin goodbye for the day.

I liked the fact that today's group was small, and the transportation offered comfort, spotless windows, and great views. I took several video shots through those windows. The tour leader arranged for several stops along the way to view or photograph the magnificent trees, quaint buildings, and vast skies. We had several free hours near Jackson Village, where I snapped dozens of colorful street photos of the locals. I couldn't wait to tell Ranger about the highlight of my day, lunch at the Red Fox Café. I hoped we could return to that spot together in the near future.

Ranger

From my office window at the ranger station, I noticed the sun had begun its downhill journey toward the horizon. Likely only five hours of sunlight remained. Finished with the day's paperwork, my least favorite task, I began to think about Autumn and wondered why I still hadn't heard from her. I was about to call again when one of my co-workers dashed in breathless and needed my help. She'd received word from one of the tower lookouts that someone had set an illegal trap, and a medium-size animal was caught in it.

Fanny, that's what I call her, though others had a different name for her, carried one of our well-stocked medical kits. I grabbed the box containing tools to disarm the trap and some rope and then went to my truck to get my gun, 'cause you never know. The animal might be beyond saving, or the culprit might return to check his trap.

Fanny and I sped off in one of the Forest Service's off-road vehicles. Fanny insisted on driving. She always said that she was a racecar driver in a previous life. Today she seemed determined to prove that, so I held on tight.

"Our patient has visitors," Fanny said as we approached the location. "Damn. You brought a gun, right?"

"Always do," I said, hoping we weren't too late. I shot into the air several times from the vehicle before moving forward. "I'd rather scare the scavengers than kill them."

Typically, I believed in letting Mother Nature take charge, but this wasn't anything natural. I couldn't let an innocent animal suffer due to a human's illegal action.

Fanny ran up to the trapped animal and examined as much of the scene as she could. The animal was thrashing around, but Fanny was still able to make an assessment. "It's a young doe likely born last spring. She's small, a little bloody, but alive."

"Let's get her leg freed up." Luckily, the deer was so small her leg fit between the trap's sharp teeth. Though caught, her leg was not crushed. Bites from the coyotes drew blood. Trembling, the young deer stood and nudged up against me.

Fanny did the same. It was like a group hug. With the deer in my lap, my co-worker cozied up closer, smelling like flowers and sweat—similar to the scent I caught a whiff of at the house when I was there with Autumn. Then Fanny whispered, "This is nice."

"No, this is a rescue." I ignored her advances as best I could. "We're going to take her in to clean up her wounds, give her something to eat, and let her rest for a few days. You drive, slowly, and I will hold her."

Handling Fanny and the deer, the next couple of hours flew by. Working with the animals that live in the forest was my favorite task. And, when I could save an animal, well, that made me feel worthwhile. However, I sensed that Fanny wanted to be more than co-workers today. Not sure what brought on this unusual change in her, but she took every opportunity to brush up against me as we tended to the deer's needs.

Running late for my evening rendezvous with Autumn, I reached for my phone to give her a call. Easier said than done because I couldn't find it. I had never been without my cell phone. I wasn't one to panic, that was not my style, but an uneasy feeling swept over me.

Mentally, I retraced my movements from the time I woke up until now. The last time I used my cell was at the cabin when I called Autumn, first on her cell and then via the Inn's number. She hadn't answered either phone, which worried me.

I drove back to the cabin much too fast, kicking up dirt and gravel the whole way. As soon as I had custody of my phone again, I'd call Autumn. She must be back at the Inn by now. Maybe she forgot to take her cell today too. That uneasy feeling faded.

"Well, look at you," I said to the visitor sitting on my porch. "Haven't seen you in a few days." Red, my friend, didn't move when I approached. "You do know you really should be wary of humans?" The small fox looked up at me, then watched me walk right by her and into the cabin.

My cell phone was right there on the nightstand. Mixed feelings rumbled in my gut. Not sure which bothered me more: going to work without my phone or that I'd let a woman distract me from my usual routines.

Heading out, I said adios to Red, jumped into my truck, and called Autumn. When no answer came, my foot pressed heavily on the gas pedal.

My fast-moving truck screeched to a sudden stop at the Inn's main entrance, a spot reserved for guests checking in. Good grief! I'm a ranger, not a cowboy. Still, I rushed into the lobby, and there she stood. We each froze, staring at the other as if we'd seen a ghost.

"Autumn?"

"Ranger?"

We rushed toward each other. Embracing, we made physical contact like something you'd see in a movie. I didn't even care if others noticed. I was relieved and happy to know that she was all right.

"I've been calling you since last night. You didn't answer your cell or your room phone."

"I know. It's kind of complicated. It seems I've lost my cell, and somehow, the room's phone had its volume turned off. Eventually, after listening to your messages, I called your phone, but you didn't answer."

"Yeah, sorry about that. I went to work and left my phone at the cabin."

"What's that old saying? All's well that ends well? At least the day is ending well." Her sweet smile melted my heart.

"Well, then," I replied, thinking I was being clever contributing to all the wells. "Let's grab a quick dinner here, then head out to the haunted house to see our horse."

Autumn took my hand and headed down the hallway toward her suite instead of to the restaurant. Maybe she wanted me to look at the malfunctioning phone. Yeah, that was probably it.

She used her keycard to open the door. "I just need three minutes to freshen up. The tour was wonderful but long and exhausting, and I want to change into my jeans."

My eyes followed her as she walked into the sleeping area, then blinked when I saw what appeared to be a large bed sheet taped to the wall. I squinted, hoping for a better look, but she had closed the door behind her. What the heck was that all about? The odd sight stalled my imagination. What was it covering? I wanted to know but felt I shouldn't ask. Maybe she would tell me about it at dinner.

Dinner didn't take long—the soup and salad went down quickly—and our conversation centered on brief descriptions of the day's events. No mention of the weird wall covering. We were both in a hurry to get back to the horse and make some progress on cleaning the house. We agreed to tackle one room at a time.

Chapter Eight

Autumn

The horse greeted us at the gate. I couldn't wait to give her the small apple I'd saved. "I'll open the gate," I said and reached for the door handle.

Ranger held my arm. "Wait in the truck."

He sounded so serious. "It's no problem. I can do it."

"I know you can. Humor me, and please, stay in the truck while I take a quick look at the horse. She should not be out wandering around."

I nodded. If I were a girl who looked in mirrors, I would see a frown and a worried expression on my face. Something was off. That much I knew. The horse seemed happy to see us, though.

"Is everything all right?" I asked Ranger when he returned to the truck.

"Not sure. We left her in the barn. And I'm pretty sure she hasn't mastered the art of opening doors yet."

"Is the coast clear enough for me to open and close the gate now?"

He nodded, but I could tell he had much on his mind. I quickly got out and opened the gate for Ranger and then swung it shut and locked it after he drove through. Back in the cab, we drove slowly toward the barn. The horse ran ahead of us, kicking up its hind legs and stopping to turn as if to make sure that we were still following her.

"Let's check the barn first," Ranger said as he pulled to a stop.

When we got out, Ranger immediately went inside the barn and I approached the horse. Finally, I was able to give her the apple I'd brought. While she chewed it, I rubbed her neck, her beautiful silky neck. She was mostly black except for a white, star-shaped mark on her forehead.

"Come on. Let's see what Ranger is doing in the barn. Maybe he's discovered your escape route."

The good news was that the double doors were not damaged. If the horse had managed to push them open, the latches would be broken. So who opened those doors? Ranger took my hand and led me over to the rustic shelf that held the horse treats. Today, it held more than that. We both stood there staring at what looked a lot like my phone.

Ranger handed it to me. Without a doubt, this was

my phone, but I did not place it on that shelf. I'd made only one call to Martin to ask for a dumpster, and I was outside at the time.

"Check it. Make sure it works," Ranger said. "Someone set your phone on that shelf and left the doors open. It's hard to say if that person had ill intentions or was trying to be helpful. Either way, I don't like it. No one had the right to be here."

I suggested we walk the property while we still had some light to make sure nothing else seemed out of place, and then we'd get to work.

Ranger held my hand while we walked, and I worked up the strength to inform him of my time frame. "In seven more days, my vacation will be over, and I'll be flying back to Florida. I assure you that the house will be almost ready for Halloween before I leave."

"Is leaving after your tenth day a requirement enforced by the sponsors of your vacation?"

I had to think about that. "I'm not sure, Ranger. But I'm pushing my luck with my parents just by being here. I wasn't exactly honest with my mother about this vacation, and neither of us informed my father, who is still on a business trip."

"Well, darlin', that sounds like one tricky situation. I don't know what to say except that I want to spend as much time with you as possible. Let's go scrub some cobwebs together."

We walked into the house together. Ranger set up a

portable CD player he'd brought in from the truck earlier, plugged it in, and hit Play.

And scrub we did for several hours to one country tune after another. I was happy to learn that the electricity had been turned on that morning. Now that we were able to work after dark, we accomplished a lot. We cleaned the main living room and dining area from top to bottom. The rooms still looked unappealing and dingy, but that would enhance the haunted look of the house.

"You know, Autumn, I prefer to think of this as a Halloween house rather than a haunted house."

"I love that idea, but aren't you required to create a haunted house? Which reminds me, where is the ghost, the werewolf, and the witch that I met the same day I met you?"

"Toward the back end of the barn."

"Let's bring them in before they get too dusty or dirty or stolen."

Ranger frowned, so I frowned right back at him. What was so wrong with my idea?

"Well? Do you have a different plan?"

"I'm working on that."

Not the answer I'd hoped for but, for now, I would accept it.

Trying to lighten the mood, I said, "Let's wrap it up for tonight. It's getting late, almost the witching hour. Ooooo."

He did not laugh or even smile. True, it was a poor

imitation of a scary sound. Did he know something I don't know? We closed up the house, took the horse to the barn, and drove back to the Sugar Lane Inn. Not a word was spoken. The awkward silence was unbearable. More determined than ever, I would get to the bottom of Ranger's unexplainable reaction to a brief segment of the evening's conversation.

He did walk me to the Inn's main entrance. All I desired from him tonight was a friendly hug. It didn't come, so I instigated that gesture before he could walk away. At least he didn't object to my boldness.

Looking up into his serious blue eyes, I said, "See you tomor—"

He placed a finger over my lips. "Yes, and by tomorrow I will find a way to tell you what's going on inside me."

"Okay." I nodded and watched him head back to his truck. I felt my shoulders slump. I'd forgotten to tell him about the highlight of my day: lunch at The Red Fox Bar & Grill.

I walked down the hallway toward my suite, went inside, quickly changed from jeans to jammies, and fell exhausted into the huge bed. Although I was snuggled in tight, sleep would not come. Recalling the last few minutes with Ranger before closing the house, I tried to figure out what I'd said that could have changed his entire demeanor. Then it came to me. His frowning began when I'd suggested bringing our trio of ghouls into the house. Then, his mood took a turn for the worst after I attempted humor by mentioning the witching hour. Was that such a bad thing? I'd heard others say that before. I had no answer to my question.

Picking up my phone from the nightstand, I opened the web browser and typed those dreaded words into its search box. I'd soon have some answers. Ten minutes later, knowing more about the witching hour, I turned on the TV and the lights in my bedroom. Lying there alone in the dark was not high on my list right now. The witching hour, which was historically from 3 a.m. to 4 a.m., now began at midnight, and midnight was fast approaching.

I don't know when my eyes finally closed, but suddenly, they were wide open, and sunlight streamed in through the cracks where the curtains were not fully closed. I survived the night, then laughed at my mini-hysteria.

What time was it? I checked my phone again. It was 6:40 a.m. Today's excursion to The Sherman Farms Corn Maize would leave in twenty minutes. Its early departure time had escaped my thoughts, and now I barely had enough time to throw on some clean clothes. I'd manage, but I'd be hungry until the tour stopped for lunch.

Dashing toward the door, I almost missed seeing the breakfast tray on the table by the window. Hmm. No time to question how it got there, but I was able to grab a blueberry muffin on my way out of the suite.

I hurried down the hall toward the lobby but stopped when I heard the desk clerk call out to me.

"Miss Reed," she said. "These flowers arrived for you early this morning. Aren't they beautiful?"

Indeed they were. "Do you mind keeping them until I return? The tour van is about to leave."

"I'd love to. Don't you want to read the—"

I was already out the door.

Chapter Nine

Ranger

It had been years since I had experienced a restless, sleepless night. And I vaguely recalled hearing a faint, though shrill screaming sound around midnight. Probably witches. I could joke about them now, but not last night at the haunted house. I was afraid I'd upset Autumn, and I hoped she wasn't too mad at me.

The sun's beams would shine through the surrounding trees soon, so I thought I might as well get up. I boiled some water, preparing to make a cup or two of instant coffee. I usually waited until reaching the Forest Service office to begin downing multiple cups of caffeine, but this morning, I needed it now. I lit a small fire in the fireplace to take the chill off. I'd be here for a while—no reason to arrive at my office early. I'd have received a call by now if there were any emergencies.

Sipping on cup number two, I heard an odd noise that sounded like a tiny scratching. I kept listening and walked softly from window to window to see if anything was out of the ordinary around the cabin. When I opened the front door, I discovered the source of the sound.

"Red!" Blood oozed from the small fox's body. "You're hurt, little buddy." Carefully, I picked her up and brought her inside before another predator detected the scent of blood. She'd be easy prey now with these injuries.

I wrapped her in one of my sheets and then placed her gently on the couch. I threw on my boots, scooped her up, and drove quickly to the infirmary next to the Forest Service office. While I was good at taking care of wildlife, others there were more qualified than me when it came to patching them up, and Red deserved the best.

I rushed into the infirmary getting more and more worried about Red. Fanny was already there feeding the recuperating animals needing a little more time before returning to the wild.

"Morning. We've got a new patient," I announced, setting Red down on the stainless steel table, gently rubbing the fox's head, and talking softly to her.

Fanny looked happy to see me despite our last encounter. I explained that I thought the fox had flesh wounds and a leg wound but no internal injuries. Until we took a closer look and performed a few tests, we couldn't be sure.

We got to work cleaning the cuts or talon marks. "Hold still, Red. You're going to be all right," I tried to assure her.

Fanny laughed. "You've taken to naming the wildlife? Tsk, tsk. Not a good idea, you know."

"Yes, I know. This one is special, though. She likes me. Even came to my door for help."

We patched up my fox and gave it some antibiotics. After a couple of quick x-rays and blood work, we made her comfortable in one of our medium-sized crates. I hung around watching her, feeling relieved that we were able to help her. It wasn't long before those thoughts strayed to my Halloween predicament.

Watching Fanny continue to feed her other charges and clean up their cages, a wild and crazy idea popped up. "Hey, Fanny, do you like Halloween? Do you ever read scary books or watch scary movies?"

"I love scary books and movies and anything with a post-apocalyptic theme. Never could get into *The Texas Chainsaw Massacre* stuff, though," she said.

I nodded at her as a smile began to form on my face.

"Slow down, Ranger. Are you asking me for a movie date?"

"No, of course not," I said with a wince. "But I might be asking for your help."

I gave her the condensed version of my unusual

inheritance and its requirements. I left out my own problems.

"You've definitely captured my attention, Ranger. This sounds exciting. What exactly do you have in mind?"

"I'm hoping you'll agree to help me set up an area dedicated to the real scary portion of the haunted house for the people that like that sort of stuff."

"Ok, sounds reasonable," she said.

"I'd like you to drive over to the house today. I'll cover for you here while you're gone. Check out the house, including the property. Come back with some ideas for this separate scary section's location and what we, I mean you, will need to make it happen. I envision today's scouting trip, a shopping trip, and a day to set it all up. So, three days of work."

"I'm in! Sounds like fun. I assume you will be with me during part of this project, right?"

I shook my head. "I have some other things to tend to," I said. "But I'll pay you well."

Fanny stalled, and I knew she was waiting for me to sweeten the deal. I groaned internally because I had no choice but to do that.

"If you're willing to show up on Halloween and help out a little, I'll take you out for a late dinner as soon as we close up that evening."

One thing was for certain, I'd regret making dinner plans with Fanny part of the deal. But with Autumn traveling home to Florida in a few days, I needed my co-worker's help. I could think of no alternative.

"Okay. I suppose I could do that," she said, sounding bored, almost disinterested.

"I have one more important request. Stay away from my horse. She's not used to strangers yet."

"Oh, I think she is. By the way, I won't need driving directions, just the keys."

Suddenly it hit me that she had already been there and didn't care that I knew. "It was you? You put the cell phone on the shelf and let my horse out of the barn?"

"I wouldn't exactly call that building a barn," Fanny scoffed.

Furious, I blurted out, "Our deal is off. I don't want you anywhere near that house or my horse."

"Come on, Ranger, let me explain."

"This better be good."

"Curiosity got the better of me when I overheard some of the guys in the break room discussing your haunted house. I just wanted to see it. When I arrived at the address, I heard a horse whinnying. So, I climbed over the gate and walked toward the sound. That's when I saw a cell phone lying in the dirt."

"Well, I call that trespassing and spying on me and Autumn."

"Who's Autumn?"

"A friend and she's none of your damn business."

"Okay. Is the deal back on?"

"Yeah, I guess so, but you must vacate the property before 5 p.m. and leave the key under the pot by the front door. Got it?"

"Got it. I'd better get going." Fanny held out her hand. "The key, remember? I do need that."

"It's under the pot I just mentioned."

What had I gotten myself into? Trouble, that's what. And all because of my past Halloween trauma. I needed to get over that. The sooner, the better.

Autumn

Even though I didn't look into mirrors, except for an occasional glance into the tiny mirror in the compact that held my face powder, I knew that right now my smile was big and beautiful. Ranger would be here soon, expecting to take me to dinner, but I had another plan for tonight. And I was all set to implement it.

As I sat in the lobby of the Inn, I watched as Ranger took the front steps two at a time and hurried right past me and over to the front desk. True, typically, he'd call my suite from the house phone to let me know he'd arrived, but maybe something was different today. Ranger turned his head my way after the clerk pointed in my direction.

I waved and couldn't wait to let him in on my surprise. It was the least I could do after receiving such beautiful flowers this morning. They must have been from Ranger, though by the time I picked them up at the front desk, the card was no longer attached.

I stood behind several large, sturdy bags watching his curious face peruse the unexpected sight.

"What do we have here?" he asked as he approached me. "Are you going somewhere?"

"Let's just say there is no need to stop for dinner. We will partake in a picnic at the haunted house. How many people can say that?"

Speechless, he merely shrugged and stared down at the bags surrounding my feet. "So, we're taking all of this with us?"

"That's the idea. We should get going and take advantage of arriving almost two hours earlier than usual." Oh, dear. His frown had returned. "Do you have a problem with that?"

"Uh, no. Just surprised. I rarely receive surprises. My days are pretty routine."

I pointed at the heaviest bags for him to grab, picked up the ones I knew I could carry, and we walked out of the lobby to load everything into his truck.

"Something smells good," he said as we got on the road.

"That's probably the chili or the garlic bread. I also brought bowls, spoons, glasses, a bottle of red wine, and a thick, warm blanket to sit on."

"How did you manage all this?"

"I had some help from the Sugar Lane Inn's chef. He's very nice. And today's excursion was only four hours long, so we got it done with plenty of time to spare. Oh, there is one more aspect of our evening I need to ask about."

"I'm listening," Ranger said with a hint of skepticism.

He probably intended to listen, though his body language begged to differ.

"Have you tried the old stone fireplace yet? Do you know if it works?"

From the distant look on Ranger's face, I concluded that he did not know and had little interest in my picnic surprise. What I didn't understand was *why*.

"I made a decision today that I think you should know about," Ranger said.

That sounded ominous. I held my breath. Did I want to listen to what he had to say?

"I decided that we must have one very spooky section or room in our haunted house. Reluctantly, I hired a friend to plan and decorate the scary area, so you and I don't have to."

I asked when this person would begin just as we approached the property's gate. Ranger got down and opened it. After he drove through, I jumped out to close it.

"Well, when do you expect help to arrive?"

"I thought today, but I see no sign of her car. Maybe I misunderstood what she'd said."

"She? Your scary, witchy helper is a woman? What's her name?"

"Uh, Fanny. She's a co-worker. I'll tell you more about her after we unpack and check on our horse."

I did remember Ranger mentioning his female co-workers in a general sort of way, though I didn't recall the details of that brief conversation.

After setting the food items and remaining bags on the kitchen counter, we hurried outside, anxious to see the horse. We made sure there was always plenty of water and hay in the makeshift stall, but when we were here with her, we put some alfalfa and a small bucket of water near the front steps so she could see us and we could see her. She liked being close to us. If we left the door wide open, I was pretty sure she'd walk right in.

As we approached the barn, she whinnied as if to say hello. As soon as we opened the double doors, she bounded out, kicking up her heels. She was a happy horse, no doubt about it. Moments later, standing side by side, we took a short, pleasant walk around the property.

"Getting hungry?" I asked.

"As a matter of fact, I am. What can I do to help?"

We quickly walked back to the house, leaving the barn doors open, so the horse could go in and out as it pleased.

I showed Ranger the cast iron pot that held the chili and requested that he check to confirm that the fireplace worked. If Ranger got a fire going, we'd eat hot chili; if not, we'd make do with a lukewarm meal.

"Now I know why one of the bags was extremely

heavy," he chuckled and pointed at the sturdy pot. "I'll check the fireplace."

Feeling happy and full of positive energy, I spread the blanket out on the floor not far from the fireplace.

"Huh," said Ranger, crouched down with his back to me. "I guess our helper was here. Complete with kindling, sticks, and a few logs, the wood is ready to light. I never asked her to do anything but scout out the best location for the spooky room and develop a plan of action to decorate it."

"Perhaps she's hoping to earn some extra credit," I said.

Ranger tuned to face me now. "You could be right."

I finished setting up the blanket as if it were a table while Ranger lit the fire. Within minutes, smoke poured into the room and we both began to cough.

"Dammit. The flue must be closed. Open the door, Autumn."

Hearing the intensity in his voice, I ran to open it. Of course, the horse was right there, but not for long. The smell of smoke sent her galloping back to her stall. I blamed myself. If only I hadn't asked Ranger to light a fire or if I'd brought sandwiches instead of chili to our picnic. This old house could go up in flames in minutes.

"I've got it. The flue is open now, and the smoke is going up the chimney as it should."

He must have noticed the panicked expression still lingering on my face because he wrapped his arms around me and said, "We're fine, really. Since we're both chilly and smelling like smoke, we'll pretend we're camping." Then he lifted my chin upward and kissed me on the lips. The chill left my body, and I could breathe again.

Ranger grabbed the cast iron pot from the kitchen and set it in the fireplace off to the side of the actual flames. There it could reheat while we checked on the horse once again.

As I rubbed the horse's neck, Ranger held her face and asked, "Hey, girl. How're you doing?" She took the treats we offered and whinnied softly. She didn't follow us back to the house, though. Smart horse.

The fire crackled and popped; it was a beautiful sight. However, having lived most of my life in Florida, I had no knowledge of fireplaces or central heating. Ask me about AC? I have experience with that. So, we kept our jackets on because most of the heat went straight up the chimney.

Although chilly, our picnic was nearly perfect and bordering on romantic. No, it was romantic. I could see it in his eyes and I felt it deep in my soul. I suppose I could be mistaken. I had read romance books—the book club chose one now and then—but never felt anything like this before.

"I've got an idea," Ranger began. "Since we have electricity now, let's look around the second floor."

"Do you think there are ceiling lights up there?" I asked. "I doubt there are lamps since the place is unfurnished."

"Let's go find out."

With a flashlight in one hand, he took my hand in his other, and up the creaky stairs we went searching for a wall switch. Cold air seemed to circle around us as we walked slowly down the narrow hallway.

"Do you feel that?" he asked.

"I do. It's kind of creepy. Perfect for a haunted house, don't you think?"

Ranger squeezed my hand. I felt safe with him so close to me.

He moved the beam of his flashlight from side to side. Still, no wall switches, though we did come upon a door to one of the rooms. As expected, it creaked as he opened it. We both laughed softly. Voila! A ceiling light fixture. Now, if only it had a working bulb in it.

"Stay put for a second," he said. "I'm going to search for a light switch."

I could barely see the outline of Ranger's body as he moved cautiously. The flashlight's narrow beam bounced around the pitch-black room.

"Found a wall switch," he said, surprised and excited.

"Let there be light!" Had there been time, I might have added a drum roll just before he flipped that old switch.

Darn. No light today. The room remained dark, too dark and cold. That's when I heard something fall to the floor.

"I dropped the flashlight! Its light went out, and now I can't see anything," he whispered.

"Me either," I whispered back.

"Do you hear that? The sound of something moving or sliding. It brushed against me!" Ranger gasped, took my hand, and said, "We're out of here."

Moving too quickly to speak, Ranger threw water on the remaining coals. We closed up the barn and drove off in the truck. Never again would we go upstairs in the dark. A more thorough clean-up would have to wait until tomorrow.

Chapter Ten

Ranger

We drove in silence for a while. What could I say? I wasn't 100% positive about what happened. It was more like an eerie feeling as if I were walking through an old graveyard on a moonless night.

Man up, I told myself. Be strong for Autumn. "I'm so sorry. I hope I didn't frighten you. I thought we'd be fine up there once the overhead light went on. When that failed, and who knows what brushed against me, I overreacted."

"I'm glad you did, or we might still be there," she said. "Instead, we're heading toward a safer, brightly lit location. Checking out that room in broad daylight needs to occur before spending any additional dark hours at the house. I will worry about the horse, though."

"She'll be fine. Now that I'm away from what spooked me, and I might know what it was, there is something else I should tell you."

I reminded Autumn of the first day we met and of the three spooks that sat in the back of my plane. Then I asked for her patience. I didn't want to dive into my Halloween paranoia while driving but promised to tell her the whole story once we arrived at the Sugar Lane Inn.

We found a quiet corner in the Sugar Lane Inn's lounge, ordered two glasses of wine—yes, I needed some liquid courage—and I began to tell my tale. One I'd never spoken of before.

"Promise you won't laugh? It's a true Halloween story."

"Of course, I promise. By the look on your face, I can tell that it's not about smiling pumpkins or candy apples."

"I have an irrational fear, a phobia really. I can thank Tom, my older step-brother, for that. He took great pleasure in creating scary pranks, and I learned, years later, that he began doing this when I was only three.

"He was a big fan of rubber bugs, spiders, and

snakes and placed them under my pillow, on my bed, even in the bathtub. But the worst prank happened on Halloween. I think I was seven. He and a buddy dressed up, one like a werewolf with huge fangs and the other like a ghost with claw-like hands. I thought they were real at the time."

I chugged the entire glass of wine as if it were water and continued.

"They came running up to me; neither made a sound. It was eerie and unbelievably frightening. The werewolf bit me while the ghost clawed at me. Blood poured out from where their fangs and claws had dug into my skin. I thought the red stuff was my real blood. I regretted going trick-or-treating by myself."

As I revealed my horrible Halloween experience to Autumn, more questions about my step-brother and step-father came to mind. I never knew either of them very well. For now, I pushed those thoughts aside.

"I didn't know it was my step-brother and his friend until much later. Even with that knowledge, I never went out on Halloween again."

Just talking about that night gave me the chills. I wondered what Autumn was thinking. She never took her eyes off me or said a word.

When I finally stopped talking, she took my hand and said, "So that's why the three passengers in your plane were covered up, huh?"

"Yes. I do everything I can to avoid triggering that

horrible feeling. I expected that phobia to go away as I grew older, but it didn't. Not yet anyway."

"Does your phobia have something to do with the woman you hired to help with the haunted house?"

I nodded, feeling somewhat embarrassed about the whole situation. Not that I was some macho guy, but I hated that I was afraid of fake ghosts, witches, and werewolves.

"Do you believe in ghosts?" Autumn asked.

I shrugged. I had no good answer. "How about you?" For some unknown reason, my question lit up her face.

"Well, during the day, I don't believe in ghosts. At night, I'm more open-minded about their existence. I did have a brief ghostly experience at the Stanley Hotel in Estes Park, Colorado, when I was on a trip with my parents. I was lying in bed when I felt a soft, silky fabric, like chiffon, sweep over me. A bit later, the window just feet away creaked open for no apparent reason. I was thrilled. The hotel was famous for its ghosts."

I motioned for the cocktail waitress to come over.

"I'll take one more," I said, pointing at my glass. Autumn raised her hand. "You too, Autumn?" She nodded. "And another for the lady."

We sat in silence until our drinks arrived. Autumn raised her glass and motioned for me to do the same. She had an uncharacteristic look of mischief on her face.

"To us and our phobias. Perhaps couples counseling is in our future," she teased.

We tapped our glasses and each took a sip.

"Did you know your fear of werewolves has a name?" she asked.

I shook my head.

"I've done a little research on phobias. It's called lupophobia."

"Huh. I didn't know that," I said.

"To our phobias," she said again. I hadn't really caught it the first time she said it, but now it made me curious.

"What do you mean by *our* phobias?"

"I have a story to tell. Like you, I hadn't planned on telling it, but this seems like the perfect opportunity."

With that, she had my full attention. I was anxious to hear what she had to say. I could not imagine her having any type of phobia.

"You don't have to do this."

"It's okay. I want to."

I took her hand and kissed her cheek. "Then I'm happy to listen."

"When I was about six years old, I was delighted to hear that a circus was coming to town, and there would be elephants and giraffes. I'd always wanted to see those animals up close. But my parents had a fund-raising event to attend, so they couldn't take me."

We each took a sip of our wine and kissed on the lips right there in public.

"They called a young woman, Sarah, who would stay with me whenever our housekeeper needed some time off. Sarah took me to the circus, and I was thrilled beyond belief. We were having a wonderful time doing everything I wanted to do until Sarah saw the house of mirrors and insisted on going inside. She took my hand, and in we went. I had no idea what to expect.

"It seemed like we were the only ones in there. With all these mirrors, Sarah couldn't resist running a brush through her hair and reapplying lip color. She dropped my hand to accomplish these things. I took a few steps, mesmerized by seeing so many of me, and turned several times, spinning like a top. The next thing I knew, I was lost, and I panicked. Surrounded by myself, I couldn't see Sarah anywhere."

"That must have been awful. How did you get out?"

"That part, I don't remember. But ever since then, I've had an irrational fear of mirrors. That too has a name: spectrophobia."

Autumn produced a small compact from her purse and showed me the mirror inside it.

"This is about all the mirror I can take without hyperventilating or trembling. I tape postcards of places we've visited to the mirror in my bathroom at home, leaving just a small portion of it showing. Weird, huh?"

"It's all weird, darlin'. Thanks for sharing that with me. We're quite a couple, each with childhood trauma to contend with."

I took Autumn's hand in mine, intending to walk through the lobby to the main exit where we would say goodnight. That was my plan until the desk clerk flapped an envelope in the air. I looked around. We were the only people in the lobby.

"That must be a message for you," I said. We both shrugged and stepped closer to the front desk, where Autumn took possession of that envelope.

"You're correct. My name's handwritten right here on the front."

She held it up to show me. I watched her open it, and then, after hesitating for a moment, she smiled sweeter than an angel. Her beautiful tawny brown eyes held a sparkle I hadn't noticed before, a far cry from her expression while telling of her mirror experience. Autumn took my hand again and led me down the hall to her suite.

Autumn

I was relieved that Ranger knew about my issue with mirrors. He could come into my room now, and I didn't need to hide the sheet. It was still ugly and weird, but at least he was aware of its purpose. We were both exhausted, and Ranger would benefit from a short, relaxing rest before driving back to his little cabin in the woods. Before opening the letter, I turned the TV to a country music channel, the volume low.

"It's from Martin," I said.

"Who?

"You know, the guy that is The Fantasy Maker's right-hand man."

Was Ranger confused, too tired to think, or just bored with this topic?

"He's the one who arranged for the dumpster. The note says he's gone back to his job coordinating other Fantasy Maker vacations. He offered to remain in my life for the duration of my fall photos vacation, but he'd do that from a distance."

"That's good because I got the impression he was lurking, watching your every move. Sometimes, our every move."

I sensed that Ranger—the saver of animals, the fire-fighter, the keeper of the forest, and a pilot—was jealous. I left out the part of Martin's note stating I could call him any day or night if any needs or problems sprung up. I figured, why add fuel to the fire?

"I think the only reason he did show up was due to the fact I was missing for a while. Nothing more. I'm sure it would be bad for business, not to mention the legal repercussions if someone harmed one of their fantasy vacation clients."

"Yeah, you're right. But is The Fantasy Maker a woman, a man, a company? Do you even know?"

Ranger had a good point. I did not know. My friends at the book club handled the entire application process, so I never gave it a second thought.

A slow song began to play from the TV. Ranger rose from the sofa, took me in his arms, and we swayed to the song "Amazed" by Lonestar. If any second thoughts planned on popping up, they didn't stand a chance. The scent of his skin and the closeness of his body pressed to mine induced a soothing dream-like euphoria. I could get used to this. If only I had more time here.

Ranger

Driving home took almost an hour, but not because it was so far. It was due to the darkness and the nature of the road. Over half of the ride was on gravel or dirt, which required driving at a speed slower than I liked. I thought about Autumn during my time alone in the truck. She was one fine lady. So pretty and sweet, sometimes I didn't know what to do or say when she was around. The few women I had worked with had a rougher, tougher edge. It was almost like being with the guys—everyone wearing similar uniforms—and it always involved Forest Service work.

Ah, home sweet home, but it wasn't. My cabin was dark and empty. Funny, that never bothered me before. What was so different now? I thought about that for a while, then it dawned on me, and I began to speak my thoughts out loud. *Glad no one was around to hear me.*

"My two foxes are missing. My temporary, red-headed girlfriend and my injured wild red fox." Unfortunately, the all-too-familiar dark and empty would be the norm before too long. I needed to stop thinking and get some rest.

I lay awake searching for a way to convince Autumn to remain in New Hampshire longer. "What, what was that?" I sat up and listened for the sound to repeat itself. I know I heard something: a thump, a punch, a tap? I had never locked my door here; tonight would be an exception.

Chapter Eleven

Autumn

Today's excursion took a dozen of us on a tour of the most idyllic New England fall festivals. I couldn't wait to tell Ranger about my successful day. I left him a phone message asking if he could arrive at the Inn earlier than we'd planned. I wanted to show him the fantastic photos on one of the desktop computers in the Inn's workroom for guests. My camera's small screen, though good, would not do them justice.

Today was also an extraordinary shopping day. That was part of the surprise for later. Now, there wasn't any room for Ranger in the living area of my suite. If he wanted to sit, stretch out, or relax, that would need to occur in the bedroom. We could make that work; there was a TV in there too. My private thoughts brought on a giggle.

I looked at my phone to check the time and see if Ranger had called or texted me. No call, no text, and he was later than usual. Should I worry? No, but I decided to order some quick to-go food from the restaurant, so we could leave as soon as he arrived. I could show him the photos another time.

Hurrying down the hallway, not watching where I was going, I bumped right into Ranger. Carrying bags and looking at his phone, he was not paying attention to what was in front of him either.

"Oops," he said, laughing. "Hi, I brought food."

"Oh, uh, good. Hang on a second," she said, stepping closer to the desk clerk, and whispered, "Can you please cancel my to-go order?"

The woman nodded and said, "Sure. No problem, Miss Autumn."

"All set, let's go. I promised the horse a special walk today, so once again, we're eating in the truck."

Ranger laughed again. "Yes, ma'am."

Once outside, I was puzzled by what I didn't see. "I don't see your truck."

"Yes, you do. It just looks different because it's pulling a trailer." He pointed toward the parking lot. Both truck and trailer were piled high with junk.

"Are you headed to a yard sale or—I can't imagine." His cargo appeared to be mostly dusty old furniture that belonged in the trash or an old, broken- down house.

Ah, ha! A cartoon light bulb hovered over my head. The items were perfect for a haunted house.

I climbed up into the truck with a little help from Ranger. Even the truck's cab overflowed with who knows what. He ran around to the driver's side and hopped in, turning the ignition as he closed the door. Once seated, he asked, "Chicken salad or tuna salad?"

I liked them both but chose the tuna. As we got on the road, I opened my sandwich and began eating. "This sandwich is good, really good," I said between bites.

"Glad you like it," he said.

The twenty-minute drive gave us just enough time to finish eating the sandwiches. We pulled up to the gate at the almost-haunted house. Here, we had a routine: He opened it, and I closed it. It worked well.

"Do you mind checking on the horse and letting her out while I unload all the haunted house furniture?"

"Happy to do that," I said as I walked to the barn. "Hey, pretty girl. I'll bet you're hungry." I knew this routine too. Though, this afternoon, I wouldn't put the extra hay and water right in front of the stairs until later. Ranger would be dragging furniture into the house right there, and I didn't want any type of collision to occur.

"Hey, you two. Where are you going?" Ranger called over his shoulder.

"Not sure, but I guess we're taking a walk. The horse is leading the way. We won't go far or be gone long."

He waved, and we walked away in a direction I hadn't gone before. The clip-clopping sound of the horse's hooves was delightful. I did learn that the stone wall did not go around the entire property. I'd assumed it did. We came upon an area where an old fence consisting of horizontal wires and vertical wood posts began and the stone wall ended. We walked along its edge until we came to a narrow gate. The horse stopped and stomped the ground with its front hoof. I didn't speak horse, at least not yet, but I knew she was trying to tell me something.

I took some photos with my phone to show Ranger when we got back. I doubted he'd been to this exact spot either. Just as I noticed a rather large pond not far beyond this fence, an eerie cold breeze brushed by me, causing me to shiver.

"I think we should go back to the house," I said to the horse. She whinnied and lay down. I'd never seen her do that before. "Come on, let's go find Ranger and some alfalfa."

She didn't budge. I went closer and rubbed her nose and ears. I took out one of the apple-flavored horse treats from my pocket. She loved those, but shook her head as if saying no. I snuggled up to her, practically sitting on her, and hugged her around the neck. She didn't want to get up, so I let her do what she wanted to do. I didn't mind. Sitting with her was very pleasant.

Caught off guard, she stood up with me halfway on her back. All I could do was hold tightly to her mane to keep from falling off and swing my leg over her as she rose. I'd never ridden a horse before and didn't know what else to do. However, she knew how to carry me home.

Ranger looked up and did a double-take as we approached. "How in the world did you manage that? I thought you lacked experience with horses."

"I didn't manage this. The horse did it all, but now I could sure use some help getting down."

"That would be my pleasure. If you're going to ride this horse, we should purchase a saddle."

"Not necessary. This was a one-time event."

Ranger had a grin on his face that just wouldn't quit. Though I enjoyed this unusual time with the horse, I found nothing humorous about it. As soon as we took a break, I'd explain what happened.

"Come take a look at what I've set up," Ranger said, looking quite pleased with himself.

In my absence, Ranger had set some hay and water near the steps. The horse seemed content to nibble on the food as we went inside.

"Wow! Did you find all this furniture at an antique store?"

"No, I got most of this from one of the Forest Service's warehouses. Years ago, when they closed up some of the cabins that had been privately leased, a lot of that old stuff was stored in there. Now we are giving purpose to that old junk."

"Well, it looks great in this haunted house."

"That's the idea, right?"

"Absolutely. Wait until you see all the colorful fall and Halloween decorations I picked up today. For now, they are taking up space in the main room of my suite. Once I set those up, this room will be almost ready for October 31."

So distracted by the look of the room, I forgot to tell Ranger about the pond and the horse's reaction. But I did ask, "How is your friend doing with the scary stuff?"

"I'm not sure. She said she wanted to keep it a secret for a few more days."

"That's odd, isn't it?"

Ranger thought for a moment. "What can I say? She's an odd woman."

"You could say, let's look around," Autumn suggested.

"Maybe, tomorrow. Let's get the horse settled in for the night."

We finished the day's goals and were pleased with our progress. I had to agree with Ranger, we were overdue for a bit of R & R.

On the drive back to the Inn, I asked, "Do you mind if I check your glove box? I think I left a pair of sunglasses there a day or two ago."

"Sure. See if there is a pack of mints in there too. And be careful of the gun. It's loaded."

My sunglasses were there, and I found the mints too. The gun didn't scare me at all, but the skimpy, black lace woman's panties did. Without giving myself any time to think, I held up the silky item and asked, "Do these belong to you? If not, who?"

Ranger slammed the brakes. Glad I had my seatbelt on.

"What the—"

"It's all right, really."

"No, it's not! I have no idea where those came from."

"Ranger, you don't owe me anything. We barely know each other, so you are free to see whoever you want to." I tried hard to believe my words.

"It's not like that. You know me better than most, and I only want to see you. I will get to the bottom of this."

Upset as I was, I felt a tiny giggle trying to escape when I heard his choice of words. As my hidden giggle faded away completely, I wondered what this all meant. An uncomfortable feeling swept through me.

Ranger pulled up at the Inn's entrance.

"I will fix this. Don't know how just yet, but I will. If this is someone's idea of a joke, it's not amusing, and I'm not laughing. If you can be ready around 4 o'clock tomorrow, I'll load up the Halloween items in your suite, and we will set them up at the house. Are you good with that plan?"

I nodded, unconvincingly, and Ranger drove off.

Chapter Twelve

Ranger

I had a hunch about the underwear culprit, but no real proof. One thought wouldn't leave my mind. I recalled hearing an odd sound the night before last. Was that the panty fairy at work? I hoped Autumn would not insist that this little mystery be solved today. I'd like to set it aside for now.

"You weren't kidding about having a room full of decorations," I said as I walked into Autumn's suite that afternoon. "You didn't need to do all this. I will pay you back someday."

"No need. I had fun selecting everything."

Although she was smiling, she wasn't her usual, perky self. I couldn't blame her. The sooner I solved the mystery the better, and I must also convince her that there are no other women in my life. Females? Yes. The horse and the fox. Women? No. Just Autumn.

When my cell phone rang, we'd only just begun unpacking and setting up Autumn's Halloween decorations at the house. The news was not good. It was also not specific. I just knew a problem had come up that needed my attention.

"I'm on my way, Fan-Tom."

"Phantom? Is that a person joking with our Halloween theme?"

"I'm needed at the Forest Service infirmary. I'll explain when I get back." Though in a hurry, I turned around and added, "Do you want to come with me?"

"I'd rather finish up here if you are certain you will be back."

"I'll return as soon as I can. It may be dark by then. Are you sure you want to stay here alone?"

"Yes. I'll be fine. If I get scared, I'll bring the horse inside the house with me."

Her words were almost amusing, but her tone was far from fine. Still, I felt I must go.

"I'll make it up to you tomorrow with a special surprise."

I think she nodded.

. . .

I jumped from my truck when I arrived at the infirmary, hoping that Red wasn't the problem.

"Whoa, you made good time," said Fanny. "The vet was here today checking on your red fox. His medical opinion was not what we usually hope for."

"And?"

"You can read his report, but the bottom line is this: The fox should not be released back into the wild. It would not survive."

I grabbed the report and went into the back room, where we kept the injured and recuperating animals. Red saw me right away. Though she didn't look so good, she smiled at me.

"Hey, little buddy. We're going to figure this out." I patted her head and began to read the report. The diagnosis was distressing, and I knew I needed to make some calls to a few surgeons. I'd hoped to have a few words with Fanny too.

"Good, you're still here," I said as I emerged from the back room.

"Yes, I was on my way out when I remembered I wanted to show you what I found."

She handed me something small, shiny, and round. I examined it and then shook my head. "I give up. What is this?"

She took it from my hand and read the words engraved on it.

"It's sort of a compact and on the cover are the words, Always Put On Your Tiara. Kind of girly, huh? I thought your new friend might like it. And check this out."

Fanny opened it up and held it out for me to look inside. The compact contained two round mirrors. Nothing else.

"Autumn has a fear of mirrors, so I double she'd want this. But thanks for thinking of her."

"Suit yourself," she said. After putting it in her jacket pocket, she departed quickly.

I should have asked where she found it. Also, I should have had the underwear conversation today.

Autumn

I kept busy decorating the two dreary old rooms—the dining area and living room—with all the new items I'd purchased, while the horse stood at the bottom of the steps nibbling on hay and watching me between bites.

"I think I've done all I can, so let's go for a short walk," I said and immediately vowed to give this beautiful animal a name before long.

I watched the sun glow orange as it dipped below the horizon, releasing its last gasp of beauty before the end of the day. Still, it wasn't dark yet. We had time to walk around the barn and then around the house. As we made our way around the house, something unusual caught my eye. I saw bright colors on the backside of the house and stepped closer to get a better look.

The horse pawed the ground like it did when we'd

walked by the gate near the pond. I gasped in shock. Someone had painted graffiti there, but it was more than just paint. It was a threat. Someone had painted a stick figure scarecrow with a snarling smile and reddish hair. The words "I'm coming to get YOU!" spewed from its mouth.

Enough is enough. Waiting for Ranger was not an option. Feeling ill, I had to get out of this place and the sooner, the better. I opened the car ride app on my smartphone and ordered a car. My parents had set up an account for me several years ago, just in case I ever became stranded. I think that applies here. Never used it before, though.

Luckily, there was a driver who could arrive in about twenty minutes. Just enough time to get the horse settled in the barn and gather up anything I needed to take with me.

I called Ranger but got no answer, so I left him a note on the kitchen table: *Returned to the Inn. Check out the back of the house.*

Ranger

Driving too fast was becoming a habit, a bad habit. Ever since Autumn came into my life, I often needed to be two places at once. No, make that three. With Autumn, at my job, at the haunted house, and now with my red fox. I guess that makes four.

Pulling up to the gate, I expected to see some light

coming from inside. There was none, not a flicker. No way would she be in that house in the dark. Did she get tired of waiting for me to return? Maybe she fell asleep.

After quickly opening and closing the gate, I began to speed to the front door. The horse must have heard my truck because she began to whinny non-stop. Was Autumn in there? I'd check the barn first.

Everything appeared to be in order. The horse was in her stall with hay and water. I gave her an apple treat and rubbed her nose. "I wish you could talk." She did seem a bit agitated, though. Something was slightly off.

Next stop, the house. I took the steps two at a time. The key was under the pot where it belonged, so I let myself in, though I doubted I'd find Autumn inside. I did find her note, though. Autumn wanted me to look at the back of the house? All right. I would check it out, then give her a call praising her work. She must have added some cool Halloween decorations back there. I grabbed the flashlight I'd left on the mantel and prepared to be pleasantly surprised.

Shocked was more like it. I was horrified at what I saw. Who would do such a thing? And why?

I ran back to my truck and called Autumn.

"Autumn, where are you?" Damn. No answer. "I'm on my way to the Inn, darlin'. I'll be there in less than twenty minutes."

I had so many questions. Had she made it back to the Inn? How did she get there? Why didn't she answer her phone? All I could do for now was hurry and worry.

I put the pedal to the metal, something I seem to be doing a lot lately.

Looking straight ahead, my eyes focused on the truck's headlights as they lit the road in front of me. I was so distracted by my thoughts that I didn't see the deer. Slamming on the brakes, the truck swerved to the side. I gasped when I heard the *thump*. Oh, God. I hit a deer. I had never done that in all the years I'd spent living and working in a wildlife area.

I got out of the truck to check the damage to the deer. It was a doe, maybe a yearling. She was still breathing, trembling but couldn't stand up. I couldn't kill her or leave her alone by the side of the road—the only two legal options—so I made my own plan. In my heart, I had no choice.

"Come on, girl," I said softly as I gently lifted her and placed her into the back of my truck. "We're going to get Autumn, and then we'll both take care of you."

I pulled up to the main entrance of the Inn, driving much slower now. I got down from the truck and nearly sprinted inside. The desk clerk had seen me and Autumn many times, so I called out to her. "Have you seen Autumn recently?"

"About half an hour ago. I helped her with the phone. The charger was her problem."

"Thanks."

I ran down the hallway and pounded on her door. "It's me. Open up. We have an emergency."

When she opened her door, I was shocked by her

appearance. She was ghostly pale with a dull stare in her eyes.

"Yes, I believe we do have an emergency. You saw it, right?"

I nodded. "Yes, I did, and we'll deal with it. For now, throw some warm clothes into an overnight bag. Is there an extra blanket in your closet?"

She nodded.

"Good, bring it. We are going to the infirmary and then to the cabin. We have a life to save."

Fortunately, she asked no questions and was ready to go in a couple of minutes. I would fill her in on the way to the Forest Service's infirmary. As we approached the truck, I took the blanket from her.

Autumn's color and energy returned the second she saw the animal.

"What happened?" she gasped.

"She jumped out in front of the truck," I said as I covered the deer with the blanket. "I couldn't just leave her lying there."

I made sure the deer was secure and then we both got into the truck. Autumn scooted closer to me and placed her hand on my thigh. "You're a good man, Ranger. The deer is the life we're saving, huh?"

I put my hand on her hand and gave it a pat before driving away. Silence reigned until we reached the infirmary. Surprisingly, the place was lit up. After closing each day, only dim nightlights flickered.

"Wait here. I'm going to see what's going on in

there. More than likely, someone forgot to turn off the main light. Still, I'm going to check."

"Fanny? I'm surprised to see you here again." I didn't see another vehicle.

"Yeah, well, I could say the same. Thought I'd recheck our two new patients and your red fox since I missed my early evening rounds. I had an extremely busy day."

She sounded angry. This co-worker had always been a little strange, and tonight was no exception. It was as if she'd been caught with her hand in the cookie jar. She seemed anxious, almost resentful. I could be wrong, and I hoped I was, but I swear she just gave me a creepy, jack-o-lantern grin.

"Okay, well, goodnight. We will talk tomorrow," I said to Fanny's back as she dashed out the door. I hurried to my truck, to Autumn and the deer, and saw Fanny speeding away. Why had she parked her car behind the building? Another question for another day.

"Was that Fanny?" Autumn asked when I returned to the truck.

"Sure was. Said she was making up for missing her morning infirmary shift today. Help me get the deer inside. When I lift her body, can you support her neck and head?"

"Got it."

We worked together and got the motionless deer inside. We laid her on a stainless steel table in the infirmary's main examination room.

"Not much blood. That's good, right?" Autumn asked.

"Maybe, but I'm concerned about internal bleeding."

We worked side-by-side cleaning a few of the deer's scrapes, squirting some water into her mouth, and then made her comfortable in the infirmary's only large holding pen.

"That's about all we can do tonight. I'll call the vet tomorrow. Fan-Tom is a good vet tech, but sometimes her skills are limited."

"Phantom? There's a Fanny and a Phantom that work here? That's too weird."

"True, especially now that we are creating a haunted house. I'll explain when we get to the cabin."

"And we'll discuss the—wait! What was that? Something moved in the hall over there," Autumn said, pointing.

"No one else is here. Maybe a bird flew in during the day and is looking for a way out."

"It seemed close to the floor, almost bouncing or hopping. I didn't get a good look, but it could have been a bird, a shadow, or my imagination. I'm a little on edge tonight."

I kept my next thought to myself for Autumn's sake. The last thing the infirmary needed was a family of rats. I walked out of the exam room to the front door and locked it so no new visitors would enter. Turning back to Autumn, I asked her to keep watch right where she was while I checked out the other rooms.

"Mystery solved," I called out from the far end of the hall. As I rounded the corner, pure joy appeared on Autumn's face.

"The red fox. What's it doing here?"

"She rumbled with a large hawk recently. It didn't go well, and now she's a patient here."

"Can I pet her? After all, you're holding the small fox in your arms and rubbing its ears. What harm could come from one more caring person's gentle touch?"

"Sure. Just remember she is a wild animal and she's injured pretty bad." I wasn't ready to tell her about Red's probable diagnosis yet. Autumn assisted me as we put the fox back in the crate where she belonged, wondering all the while how she got out. *Hmm. It seems I may have a foxy fox.*

"Time to go build a warm fire at my cabin. What do you say?"

"I say, let's go. We still have several topics to discuss."

"Yes, indeed we do."

Chapter Thirteen

Autumn

I snooped around the small kitchen, looking for something to eat. I wasn't hungry earlier, but now my gurgling, empty stomach was hard to ignore. The shelves held cans of soup, some pasta, and chocolate protein drinks. The fridge was even bleaker.

I watched Ranger build a fire, then asked, "Are you hungry?"

"Yes, very hungry. Unfortunately, this was such a busy day, and I had not foreseen us spending the night here, so there's not much to choose from. Do you want to take a drive in search of a meal?"

"No. We could heat up a can of soup, but that's about it. Nothing in the fridge to speak of."

"Did you check the freezer? I might have frozen some leftovers a few days ago."

There was hope. He had cooked two TV dinners for us the first night I was here at his cabin. Right now, any hot food would be fine with me.

I opened the freezer and, right away, saw it contained a family-size carton of lasagna. "I see that you like Italian food."

"Sure. Doesn't everybody? What brought that topic up?"

"The contents of your freezer," I said, removing the carton and turning it over to read the heating instructions. A hand-written note hid the instructions. The words there were hard to miss: *Hey lover, give me a call and I'll come right over to help you with the first course.*

A bit dazed, no words came to me. Then, "Who do you know that calls you lover?"

Ranger glanced up and laughed. "Uh, no one. What does that have to do with dinner?"

"Everything," I said, handing him the note.

He wasn't laughing now, and neither was I. Adding this to my mental list of things to discuss, I blurted out, "First, the underwear mystery, second, a threatening scarecrow, and now a mysterious lover that brings you dinner. Can you explain any of this?"

"No, not yet, but I will soon." He tossed the note into the fire.

"You just destroyed evidence."

Obviously, my words did not register with him. He said, "It is strange, and means that someone was here in my cabin recently."

The box did not seem tampered with, so I removed the lasagna from its carton and placed it in the oven to cook. We both needed to eat something.

"Maybe you should lock the truck and keep your cabin locked too until some of this weirdness is figured out."

He nodded his agreement, though his face held an angry scowl as he headed outside. I found two small, single-serving bottles of red wine in one of the cupboards and a glass for each of us. Ranger returned, and I noticed that he did lock the door, probably for the first time ever.

Sitting in front of the fire, we sipped the wine while our dinner cooked for forty-five minutes.

"Where do you want to begin?" Ranger asked.

"With the scarecrow graffiti. Someone who knows me or has seen me must have created it. They knew I had reddish-gold hair and even got the length right."

Ranger stalled. "That might be a coincidence."

No way, I thought, but moved on. "The only coincidence on my mind now concerns Fanny and Phantom. You agreed to help me understand who they are."

"They are one and the same. I called my co-worker Fanny around you, but almost everyone I work with calls her Fan-Tom."

"Phantom? Like an apparition, a spirit, a ghost?"

"I hadn't thought of it that way. My mind avoids dwelling on ghostly things, although I see why you might, considering the circumstances we are both caught up in. Her real name is Francine Thompson, which was shortened to f, a, n, t, o, m. Fan-Tom."

"Well, the other spelling works better for me. She is a bit of an apparition, a jealous one."

I summed up my own mental investigation—that Fan-Tom was responsible for the black panties in the glove box, the scarecrow on the house wall, and the love note on the carton of lasagna, though I couldn't prove any of it. Or did Ranger have a secret admirer that neither of us suspected? Whoever it was hoped to scare me away. The timer for our dinner dinged. Ah, saved by the bell for now.

I loved the lasagna despite the chilling note attached. And I definitely liked the man sitting beside me. He was kind and helpful and so ruggedly handsome. When he looked at me with those clear blue eyes and mussed-up light brown hair, Ranger reminded me of Jack in the *Virgin River* series. I wondered if I reminded him of Mel, Jack's love interest. Our hair was almost the same color, though mine was slightly shorter. We were both intelligent and nice. Mel was a very skilled nurse . . . but what was I? I couldn't answer my own question.

"A penny for your thoughts," Ranger said, tucking a loose strand of hair behind my ear.

I smiled. "I'm a little tired, that's all."

"Really? It sure looked like you were deep in thought."

I couldn't lie to this man. So, I confessed to

wondering about who I really was. Up until now, I was my parents' well-behaved daughter and a member of a book club. That was it. Hearing my admission was embarrassing.

"Huh. You're much more than that to me. You're intelligent, resilient, creative, and brave."

"Brave?"

"Yes, considering your upbringing, you took on quite an independent adventure coming from Cape Coral to this," he said, scanning the small cabin's living area.

Ranger wrapped his arms around me and whispered, "You're beautiful too."

I swear I felt my heart skip a beat. Though I thought that was merely a romance novel saying. I never had a boyfriend before. Was Ranger to be my first? He was a boy—no, he was a man—and he had acted like a devoted friend over the past week. Did that make him my boyfriend?

I watched Ranger as he added more wood to the fire. He also went outside to bring in more. I hadn't seen him do that before. "It's going to be unseasonably cold tonight," he said.

"This sofa is a sofa bed, isn't it?" I asked.

He nodded. "I've never opened it, though. When it gets super cold, I sleep out here but didn't need to open for myself."

Ranger had said I was brave, and now I was about to

prove it. "Tonight, we will open the sofa bed and sleep by the fire together."

"I'll be just fine in the bedroom. I'm used to being cold."

"No. I insist. I wouldn't be able to sleep or forgive myself knowing you were freezing while I enjoyed the warmth of the fire."

Ranger

We both stood staring at the sofa. Autumn with a look of anticipation, me with a fast-beating heart. I was slow to show enthusiasm for her idea or to begin opening up the sofa and turning it into a double bed for the night. Autumn was quick to give me the third degree regarding my hesitation.

"I don't get it. Why don't you like my idea? Do you have a girlfriend who would object, or do you snore, or maybe you think I might snore?"

She looked at me with innocent eyes waiting for a reasonable reply. I didn't have one, at least not one I was willing to share tonight.

"Well, it's getting late, and we need to be on the road early in the morning," I said. "Let's get this bed made, so the sleeping can begin."

That's all it took to make her happy.

Now, instead of staring at the sofa, we stared at each standing there fully clothed. I knew what I was thinking, but I wasn't sure about Autumn. So I followed her lead. When she took off her boots, I took mine off. Next, she removed her warm, bulky sweater. I wasn't wearing a sweater, so off went my shirt. Not having many layers on, I couldn't keep up.

I excused myself to the bedroom, where I located some flannel boxers and a tank top shirt. If we'd been playing strip poker, I would have lost by now. I went back to the living area and saw that Autumn had ended her disrobing wearing a top and some skin-tight pants. She told me the top was a cami and the pants were leggings.

"You first, my lady."

She slipped between the sheets, and I soon followed, covering us both with two wool blankets.

"Mmm, this is nice, cozy," she said softly with her eyes half-closed and a sweet smile on her face.

"I agree. Your idea was unexpected but brilliant. Want to hear about my plans for tomorrow?"

"Of course, I do."

"If you can wrap up your scheduled excursion by one o'clock, I'll pick you up and take you to lunch. Then, we're heading to the skies for some aerial photography."

Autumn sat up and held my face. "You, Mr. Lee, are the most wonderful man in the world."

Staring deep into her sleepy eyes, I got lost in them. Lost in their beauty and the mesmerizing effects that they had on me.

Uncertain of what my next move should be, I said, "Big day tomorrow. We'd better get some rest."

"You're right," she said, inching back under the covers and rolling onto her side.

I snuggled up behind her, and soon we were fast asleep.

Chapter Fourteen

Autumn

The sky was still dark and the temperature freezing as we drove up to the Sugar Lane Inn's entrance the next morning. Ranger thought he was dropping me off, but I had a plan of my own.

"Don't leave yet, Ranger. I'll be right back."

"But, I—"

He told me on the drive over that he'd spend the morning working at the house and checking on the horse. He didn't know that I was going to join him. I called room service and ordered two coffees and four chocolate donuts to go. Then, I threw another set of warm clothing, including jeans, gloves, a knit cap, and an extra sweater, into a large tote bag and hurried down the hall.

"Here you go, Ms. Autumn," the concierge said.

"Thank you."

I ran to meet Ranger, breathless as a relay racer in the Olympics.

"What have we here?" he asked with a smile as I hopped into the truck.

"Coffee, donuts, and me." I had to admit that I felt pretty proud of myself.

"You know, I really must get going."

"Uh, huh. And I am going with you to help with the house, so don't even try to stop me."

"But you will miss whatever The Fantasy Maker has planned for you this morning."

I nodded. "Exactly. Now tell me why your handsome face is cringing as if you'd just eaten a lemon. Are you okay?"

"I'm fine."

"You don't look fine. Come on, Ranger. What's up? Tell me before my imagination goes wild and thinks you have a secret meeting with The Fan-Tom."

"All right. You asked for it. Just saying, The Fantasy Maker is creepy, even cringe-worthy. The more I think about it the more it doesn't sound real or legitimate. All we know is that Lurch shows up now and then."

"His name is Martin, and he's very helpful, like a behind-the-scenes cruise director. Nothing to worry about."

I set the donuts on the center console and handed Ranger his cup of coffee. Lifting my cup, I said, "Here's to the horse and haunted house. Ready or not, here we come."

The past twelve hours had super-charged my positivity, and I knew today would be even better. Dozens of upbeat, happy tunes came to mind. Today, those songs remained within my head, but I'd sing them all out loud if I were alone.

After arriving at Ranger's haunted house, we finished our gate routine in record time, and drove in. Nothing about the property looked out of place or disturbed, so I headed over to the barn while Ranger went to open up the house.

"Good morning," I said to the horse. She whinnied and shook her mane. I opened her stall to allow her the freedom to walk wherever she pleased. "I've decided that I would think seriously about a name for you today. For now, here is an extra flake of hay and some alfalfa."

She followed me as I walked over to the house. I kissed her velvety nose before hopping up the steps. The door wouldn't open. Had Ranger locked it from the inside after he'd gone in?

"Ranger? Are you in there? Open up." I knocked and then pounded. This made no sense. I checked under the pot where we always left the key. No luck. I turned my back to the door with the intention of walking around the exterior of the house when the door creaked slowly open.

It was Ranger. How did he get in?

"Autumn, do you have the key?" Ranger stood there with a frown on his face.

"No. Don't you?"

He shook his head. "I meant to put it back under the pot last night, but now I'm not sure if I even locked the door. I was in a hurry to get to you. Hopefully, I misplaced it or left it in a pocket."

Or maybe Fan-Tom was up to something once again. I didn't say those words out loud, but I screamed them in my head.

"Well, Autumn, we're in now. Where do you want to start?"

"Since the main living area is finished except for real pumpkins, which you will need to purchase, carve, and add later, let's create a maze-like path so the guests don't trip over each other in the dark."

"The dark?"

"Of course. Not pitch black, but the lighting in this haunted house needs to be very dim and shadowy. We could use one low-voltage night-light for this room. I'll look for some green or blue bulbs later today."

Ranger thought that was a good idea. One we would try out the next time we were here after dark. Then it dawned on me. I won't be here at the haunted house, or the Sugar Lane Inn, or with Ranger much longer. Today was already the seventh day of my fantasy vacation. I hadn't planned to have so many adventures and meet such a wonderful man. *Snap out of it,* I told myself.

"Autumn, what's the matter?"

"Nothing," I said, but the expression on my face must have betrayed me. Ranger wrapped his arms around me and lifted my chin. Our eyes met, and without words, we communicated a connection, a closeness. I laid my head on his chest and he held me for quite a while. If only this moment could last forever. Going back to Cape Coral would be more challenging than I'd imagined.

We spent the next couple of hours creating a railing using ropes, dowels, some duct tape, and a heavy-duty staple gun. However, this created a new problem. Now, anytime we needed to walk through the room, we had to follow the maze or crawl under the ropes. Perhaps we should have set this up last.

Ranger reached out and took my hand. "Let's take a quick look at the dining room to see what else we might need there."

"I think it lacks only the three passengers that rode in your plane the day we met. I heard you say they were in the barn, but now I'm confused. Didn't you think they might be on the second floor?"

"Yeah, maybe. I don't remember taking them up there, though I do recall our little upstairs adventure. No matter where the three ghouls are, I'll add them to the dining area the day before Halloween."

"All right. In the meantime, we can string up the bags of spiderwebs, bats, and glowing green eyes that I brought over the other day. I think we should get some black butcher paper too, and a CD of Halloween spooky sounds, and—"

"Whoa! I get it. I'll have a shopping day in my future."

"Or I could shop back in Cape Coral and ship the items to you."

"I'm not ready to think about you being anywhere but here with me."

I didn't know what to say. Ranger looked so solemn and sad. So, for now, I said nothing and tossed him a bag of spiderwebs.

Side-by-side, we worked diligently until Ranger said, "Time to close up and go. We have lunch reservations at The Golden Leaf Cafe. After that, we'll swing over to pick up your camera and then drive to my plane."

"I can't wait! This is going to be a great adventure for me!" My smile was so big, I could feel it in my cheeks.

"You bet it is."

Ranger

We sat at a small table for two in the restaurant's garden patio.

"Nice to see you, Ranger. It's been a long time," said the server, looking briefly at me until his eyes turned toward Autumn. "I don't believe I know you. People call me Thomas."

"I'm just visiting for a few days." Then out of the blue, she asked, "Is Thomas your first name or your last?"

I wondered about her question. It seemed odd to me. Now I was curious about his answer. After all the years I'd known him, though casually and only as a server, I had never asked him about his name, and he'd never mentioned it. Or maybe I'd just forgotten.

"Huh. You are the first person to ask about my name. Actually, I go by my last name with a slight modification." Then he whispered, "I never liked my first name. Disliking names sort of runs in our family."

I knew Autumn wouldn't leave it at that.

"What can I get you to drink?"

I ordered an iced tea for myself, and Autumn asked for the same. We sat in silence until Thomas returned with our drinks. Was she thinking what I was thinking? Maybe, though the odds of such a coincidence were not in our favor. Still, it deserved some attention.

"Here you go," Thomas said as he placed our teas in front of us. "Are you ready to order, or would you like more time?"

I jumped right in with my answer. "Yes, we are in a bit of a hurry. What are your specials today?"

Thomas rattled off the three specials quickly. We both chose the grilled chicken lunch special. I was hungry and my lunch disappeared quickly, but Autumn kind of picked at her food.

"You're not eating much. How come?" I asked.

Autumn shrugged. "I thought it might be safer. The less in my stomach while we are high above the earth, the better."

Smart woman. I hadn't thought of that. She is a novice when it comes to flying in a small plane, and we will be changing altitude and making more than a few turns.

Thomas returned. "Can I get you anything else?"

"Yes, as a matter of fact you can," Autumn said. "What's your real name, first and last." She gave him one of her irresistible smiles.

He bent down and whispered something into her ear.

Autumn smiled up at him. "Thank you."

"Check, please. We need to go."

"We really do because Ranger is going to help me take some aerial—"

I could be wrong, but I had an odd feeling about this guy today and didn't want him to know our plans. Thankfully, Autumn stopped speaking when I squeezed her knee under the table and forced a smile on my face at the same time.

For a guy who had so little experience dating or relationships with women, I felt proud of myself every time Autumn smiled or laughed. I swear her tawny brown eyes sparkled all through lunch. She was her beautiful, curious, and polite self.

Back in the truck, I had to ask, "So? What is his full name?"

"His answer was complete. He said his last name was Thompson. And that his first, which he hated, was Franklin."

"I always thought he looked familiar, reminded me of someone. At the very least, it's worth investigating."

The sudden look on Autumn's face told me we were on the same wavelength. And then she said, "So Franklin Thompson and Fanny/Francine Thompson could very well be related."

"We can't be certain, but until we are, neither one needs to know what we're doing and where we're going. Agreed?"

"Yes, I agree. Are we being paranoid?" Autumn asked.

"No, we're being cautious. And I think Fan-Tom is the cause of some of the weirdness at the house. Or else the house really is haunted." I smiled weakly.

I regretted my comment, though I meant every word. Still, I should have kept them to myself. I had no proof, just hunches.

"Is it possible to open my side window? My photos might look better if they're not shot through glass."

"No, sorry, darlin'. But I did make sure all the windows were ultra clean. Your photos will be fine if you press your camera lens against the window."

"All right. I'll try that, and I will hold my camera

very still. So no bumps, jiggles, or rough winds, got it?" she said with a teasing twinkle in her eyes.

"I'll do my best. Buckle up. Here we go."

The entire time we were off the ground, the air was calm; it felt as if we were floating. I loved hearing Autumn's oohs and ahhs and descriptions of the views below and the colors in the sky as clouds rolled in, creating a magnificent light show. The landing was a little rougher than I expected. Not sure why.

"Ranger, I can't thank you enough," she said as I helped her down from the plane. "Do you mind if we take a selfie with your plane in the background? I can do that with my phone."

"Okay, sure."

It took only a second. Autumn showed me the photo and said, "It's perfect."

I had to agree we did look like a perfect and happy couple. Now, with our feet on the ground, she gave me a hug and a kiss on my cheek. We remained in an embrace, and I wondered who would let go first. It wasn't going to be me. Holding Autumn in my arms, her head against my chest, I wanted to kiss her more than anything.

I was about to do just that when a truck pulled up next to us. A quick kiss on Autumn's forehead would have to do for now. The driver lowered his window and looked out at us with a smile.

"I watched your plane land and thought I'd stop by. I'm covering for Doc Swenson," the driver said. "I received a call to check on a couple of the animals in the infirmary, and was told a key would be under the mat. I think I got turned around. Can you give me directions from here?"

"Sure," I said. "Go back down the way you came. Take the first right turn you come to, drive about half a mile, and you're there."

"Thanks. I'll only be there a few minutes."

I watched the car turn around and drive away. That encounter left me with a strange feeling. I knew Doc was getting up there in age and always wanted to be home before dusk set in, but what animal couldn't wait until morning? Had something happened today while I was gone? Fanny should have called me. Where was she now?

I couldn't leave it at that. "Autumn, we need to swing by the infirmary. It won't take long."

The vet was already on his way out as we arrived. "Everything seems okay in there," the vet said, frowning. "Water. All the animals needed was a little more water. Odd, huh? A miscommunication, I suppose. Got the impression the deer and fox might be waiting for surgery. That is not my specialty. And if it were, I wouldn't do that at night without an assistant. Sorry, but I still have to bill for an after-hours call. Good night."

Very odd, indeed. All I could think of was that someone missed their shift or part of it and didn't want me to know. I went inside anyway to make sure everything was as it should be, and I'd make a few calls tomorrow to find out who had summoned the vet.

Autumn

I could not have asked for a better day. Ranger didn't drop me off at the entrance of the Sugar Lane Inn; he parked his truck and walked me in. We held hands through the lobby and down the hall until we reached my suite. Would I receive a good-night kiss before he headed home?

Arriving at the door, I turned to face him, hoping he'd take the hint. Before I could say anything, he leaned in and kissed my lips, gently at first. I dropped my bag and put my arms around his neck. With our bodies pressed together, passionate kissing began.

"We should go inside," I whispered, short of breath and panting like a puppy. I retrieved the key card from my pocket; Ranger took it from my hand and opened the door. Our bodies and lips were still pressed together as we made our way to the sofa. Eventually, we did come up for air.

We took a break to catch our breath. I popped some popcorn in the microwave and filled two glasses with ginger ale. We munched and sipped side by side until Ranger wanted to talk.

"Because of you, we're ahead of schedule at the haunted house, and I have until October 31 to finish any loose ends. So, here's the deal, and you cannot say no."

"All right. Yes, yes, yes," I said with a giggle.

"I haven't told you what the deal is yet."

"I know, but I'm feeling beyond agreeable right now."

"I like the sound of that, so here goes. Tomorrow, I want you to relax and enjoy one of The Fantasy Maker's activities, but I will pick you up at 3 o'clock sharp, and you must be ready. I have a little surprise for you," he said confidently.

Ranger had something up his sleeve for sure, but what? My curiosity could wait no longer. "I need a little hint to dress appropriately for the occasion."

"Hmm. Anything you'd like as long as it's warm. We'll be outside."

"I can hardly wait."

"Darlin', I hate to admit it, but I'm tired. Mind if I take a short nap before driving home? I'm having trouble keeping my eyes open."

I reached for his hand and led him into the bedroom. He kicked off his boots and laid his head on the pillow.

"I'll be right back. Just going to get a bottle of sparkling water for us."

When I returned, he was fast asleep. So I put on my long, pink, silky nightgown, kissed his forehead, and curled up beside him.

Chapter Fifteen

Autumn

I'd slept better than ever and awoke refreshed, ready for this new day. Ranger was gone, though I wasn't surprised. In fact, I don't know how he had kept up with his forest rangering, the haunted house decorating, and keeping an eye on the horse, the deer, and Red—not to mention all the driving back and forth . . . and us.

Us. I liked the sound of that.

My cell phone dinged with a text message. Not fully awake yet, I reached for my phone and took a quick look. *Check the hall. See you later.*

Check the hall? I was wide awake now. What was he up to now? More flowers? That would be too much. Still, I was anxious to find out and went straight to the door, flung it open, and there was a vase filled with flowers, dead flowers, and nothing else. Paralyzed by the sight, but only for a moment, I brought the ugly flowers into my suite.

I snapped a photo with my phone, emptied the water—who waters dead flowers?—threw them into the trash and began composing a note to the gifter. *May you rot in hell just like*—No, that was so not me. I kept at it, though, hoping to create the perfect threatening note with a side of dread. *May you soon become shriveled, ugly, and as dead as your gift.* After taping my brief note to the vase, I set it back out in the hall. Two could play this game.

Now behind schedule, I quickly showered, dressed, and looked forward to today's excursion to visit some of New Hampshire's historic buildings, including churches and farms. Once I applied my mascara and lip gloss and packed my tote bag with my camera equipment and my small purse, I'd be all set to go and stop thinking about dead flowers for a while.

That's when I heard someone knocking on my door. I also expected to hear someone say *Room Service* or *Housekeeping*, but no words came.

"Who is it?" I asked.

"County Sheriff. Open up."

"Uh, just a minute." I ran to the room's phone and called the front desk.

"There is a man at my door, and he says he's with the sheriff's department. Did you see him come in?"

"Yes, Ms. Autumn, I did. He is the local law enforcement."

"Okay, thanks." Something awful must have happened. My only connections this far from home were Martin and all the tours, the Inn, the haunted house, and Ranger. Oh, dear. I peeked out the peephole. What else could I do?

"Ms. Autumn Reed? I have a few questions to ask you."

I opened the door wide enough for him to enter. "Is this about Ranger? Has something happened?" I felt myself trembling.

"No, this is about you and your death threat."

"My death threat? You must be mistaken. I didn't make a death threat."

"Who do you want dead?"

"No one. I don't want anyone dead."

The man, this ultra-serious sheriff, looked down at his phone and said, "Does *May you soon become shriveled, ugly, and as dead as your gift* sound familiar?"

"Yes."

"I ask again, who do you want dead?"

"I don't know."

He shook his head. "Maybe you'll remember better at the local precinct."

The next thing I knew, I was sitting in the back of a cop car, and for what? Writing a stupid, pay-back note? I couldn't believe that was a crime. Maybe this was a joke, a prank. I had seen those on TV. It felt real, though. I didn't want to bother Ranger, and I wasn't going to call my mother, but I needed to talk to *someone*. I decided to call Martin. He'd said to call day or night if I ever needed anything.

I tapped his number into my smartphone, and he answered right away. I explained everything from Ranger's message about checking the hall to riding in the back of the sheriff's car.

"Are you sure the message was from Ranger?" Martin asked.

"I assumed it was, but now that you've asked, I'm not positive. Even if he sent the message, he would not leave dead flowers. He's not capable of making a mean joke."

"Sounds like someone should be arrested, but it's not you. I'll make a few calls. Don't worry, Autumn. That officer is in more trouble than you are. They can't arrest you for writing a note, but they can discipline the officer. Be patient. A car will come by to take you back to the Inn."

"Thank you so much. I'm feeling better already."

Within an hour, I was back in my suite. I had missed the morning excursion, so I began scrolling through the photos I'd taken so far, deleting the ones I didn't need to keep. The selfie of Ranger and me caught my eye. We looked so good together. I'd wait until he picked me up to relate this morning's unwanted adventure, but I did have a question for him, so I sent him a text message.

Me: *What should I have found in the hall?*
Ranger: *I don't know. Food? Flowers?*
Me: *What kind?*
Ranger: *Still don't know. Fall colors would be my choice.*
Me: *Dead or alive?*
Ranger: *Huh? Sounds like a trick question.*
Me: *Never mind. I'll explain later.*

Happy and relieved to see Ranger, I threw my arms around him when he picked me up. Already, this had been quite a day; one I'd like to forget. I looked forward to a lovely evening with Ranger and maybe the horse. Come to think of it, he never mentioned where we were going. All he said was we'd be outside.

"So?" Ranger asked.

"Uh, so what?" I said slowly.

"That was an odd text you sent today. It kind of caught me off guard. Want to explain?"

"Yes, I do, but I'll need to give you the short version for now."

I recognized the route Ranger drove and knew we'd soon be at the house. I didn't want the details of my day to ruin our special evening.

"I received a text and assumed it was from you. It said, check the hall, so I did. That's when I found a vase of black, dried-up, dead flowers. Of course, that angered me, so I wrote a note, taped it to the vase, and set it back out into the hall."

"That's awful, darlin'. You didn't see anyone or hear anything?"

"Not until later, when a policeman was at my door accusing me of threatening someone's life."

We had arrived at the house. The details of my day? To be continued later. No gate duty for me tonight. It was already open, and I saw several vehicles parked by the house. "Why all the cars and trucks? It's not Halloween."

"I invited a few friends over to help out today."

"What do we need help with?"

"Dinner, a bonfire, stuff like that."

"I take it you found the key?"

"No, actually, I left the door unlocked knowing the guys would be here early in the afternoon. Don't give me that look. I hadn't found the key before we needed to head out yesterday."

"That look may be gone, but the thought is not. So, all this extra help is your 'little surprise'?"

Ranger did not answer my question but drove on and parked the truck close to the barn. He led me into the barn before I could get a good look at his friends to determine what activities they were engaged in.

Ranger's beautiful horse stood majestically outfitted with a navy blue saddle blanket, a tan saddle, and reins. "Does this mean you'll keep the horse, ride her, and—wait. When did you have time to purchase all this?"

"I have people," he grinned, "and I wanted to make sure you got to ride her comfortably a few times before you left. It's much easier with a saddle than riding bareback."

The horse and I were the only females here tonight. That was fine with me. Ranger insisted that I hang out with the horse-with-no-name while the men set everything up. I was not allowed to lift a finger.

"What exactly is going on, Ranger?"

"This event is multi-purposed. I wanted you to meet some of my ranger buddies who happen to be tough dudes and will make certain no keys go missing, no graffiti gets drawn, or no mysterious pranksters show up. I refrained from mentioning the panties."

"What about the guy over by the rock wall taking photos?"

"That's Cliff. He's a local PI doing a little investigating for me. I want everything to be perfectly safe tonight . . . and always. We still have a few lingering mysteries to solve."

"We sure do." I almost finished the story about being carted away in a cop car, but he'd gone to so much trouble to create this special evening that I didn't wish to rain on his parade right now. I'd reveal more details later.

"Tonight, we'll toss all our troubles away, right?" I said, sounding as cheerful as I could.

"Right, because this is your night, a thank you for all your help. I would have given up without you. After tonight, I want you all to myself for the duration of your time here in New Hampshire. Thus, the early celebration."

"Thank you, Ranger. Sometimes, I can't believe you're real. You are so good to me."

From the barn's open doors, I watched Ranger's friends set up tables, folding chairs, and the makings of a future bonfire.

"I hope you're hungry. The caterer will arrive any minute now."

Ranger was correct. Before he could explain the menu, a catering van drove in, and a man who resembled a cowboy began to set out a container of barbequed ribs and chicken, potato salad, baked beans, and corn on the cob. The aroma was to die for. No apparitions tonight, just a bunch of park rangers and a lot of food.

"Let's eat!" Ranger called out. "Come on, Cliff. You too." And with that a short line quickly formed.

Once everyone's plates were full and each friend had taken a seat, Ranger said he wanted to make a toast.

"Raise your cans high. Tonight is for Autumn, an amazing, talented, and beautiful woman. Without her, I never would've taken on this bizarre inheritance project and I'd be a lonely man. To Autumn."

"Hear, hear," the group shouted.

Ranger kissed my lips in front of everyone. Overcome with emotion, my eyes filled with tears. I didn't dare blink or they'd roll down my cheeks. Still, I was able to speak, although softly. "I never knew there was such a thing as a beer can toast."

Ranger laughed. "Oh, yes. There definitely is. Can I assume this is your first?"

"Uh huh. Along with several other firsts I've had this past week."

The food disappeared quickly, and the rangers gathered around the blazing bonfire bringing the cooler of cold beer with them. Even sitting close to the fire, my backside was chilled, and I was grateful Ranger had suggested I wear warm clothing.

Cliff kept his distance, and I wondered why. Another topic Ranger and I could talk about later. For now, I joined in with the group's sing-a-long accompanied by Ranger playing the guitar. I was in awe of his strumming, his singing? Not so much. What else didn't I know about him?

At the end of "Down in the Valley," he took his phone from his jacket pocket and stared at it for a moment. "Hey, everybody. Just got a long text message from Fan-Tom."

Every member of the group groaned at this news. "If she got wind of this party, I'm guessing she's damn pissed that she wasn't invited," one ranger said, and the others nodded and laughed.

"Probably, but here is what she wrote: 'I've added a few things to the "scary" room. It's almost finished. Wait until you see the Halloween mural that a friend of mine made. You and Autumn should take a look.'"

"Are you game?" Ranger asked.

I shrugged, not excited about looking at scary things in the dimly lit barn, and I was pretty sure Ranger wasn't either.

"I'm game if you're game," I said. "Besides, I think your friends want a preview of your haunted house."

"Our haunted house," he corrected.

Ranger and I led the way. We entered through the front of the barn since those doors were already open. Then through the small door that led to the walled-off back area. Yeah, this was looking good and scary back here. "It's too scary for me, but some folks will love it. I don't see a mural, though." I turned toward Ranger and shrugged.

"Maybe it's on the outside back wall of the barn," Ranger added. "Come on, guys, follow me.

Aha! We found it. A huge tarp covered about half the wall. Anticipation vibrated through the group. One ranger stated that he felt like he was attending an art exhibit unveiling a new artist's work. Another said, "If only we had a drum roll. Come on, Ranger, yank the damn tarp off."

I noticed Cliff standing off to the side, his camera aimed at the tarp. The man was all business, for sure.

Then, to add a little drama, Ranger said, "Give me a countdown from three."

"Three . . . two . . . one . . . Off with the tarp." Then silence.

I gasped and began to hyperventilate, but I couldn't turn away from the reflective monstrosity. Though my head buzzed and my vision blurred, faint comments from the men were unmistakable.

"What does this huge display of mirrors have to do with Halloween?"

"Someone went to quite an expense."

"I must ask you all to go back to the bonfire and don't touch anything," Cliff added.

I vaguely registered the rangers moving toward the bonfire. Even in my altered state, I could feel mysterious tension permeating the air, and the festive mood disappeared.

I must have passed out because the next thing I remembered was Ranger comforting me in the backseat of the truck with the help of two pillows and a blanket that he kept in the storage compartments.

"I'm ok. You don't need to make such a fuss," I said as I tried to sit up.

"Yes, I do. Can I get you anything?" Ranger's voice was nearly panicked.

"Get me away from here."

"I will. Soon. Good men surround you, so you're safe."

When I was finally able to sit, I looked out the window and saw that the area in front of the house had become an active command center.

Though my body trembled and my thoughts swirled, my ability to hear was uncanny. Ranger was over by the house, and I heard him ask for two volunteers to stand guard and stay the night. One had game cameras in his truck and was in the process of putting them up. The flurry of activity heightened the anxiety that grew inside me. I had to get away from here. Now!

The horse whinnied loudly. Then, it hit me. She was already saddled and merely a few yards from me, I could do this. The horse would be my four-legged guardian angel and take me away.

Ranger

"How is your gal Autumn doing? Seeing these mirrors sure upset her," Cliff said as he helped me tack the tarp back up to cover the mirrors.

Personally, I wanted to smash the wall of mirrors into a million pieces, but Cliff vetoed that. He treated the property as if it were a crime scene. Who knows, maybe was.

"Yeah, she's had a few rough days. The oddness of the mirrors got to her, and I'm beginning to think this house was haunted long before the decorations arrived."

"I'll take another look around before I leave tonight."

"Thanks, Cliff." The young man assured me he'd check the entire property first thing in the morning and suggested I post a few No Trespassing signs. I helped the guys pack up. We all wanted to call it a night.

"Uh, Ranger. She's gone," Cliff said under his breath.

"What do you mean gone?"

"When I went past your truck and noticed she was no longer there, I quickly looked around. No sign of her. The horse is gone too."

"Keep looking. I'll ask others to do the same."

I must have called Autumn a hundred times as I drove around looking for signs of her or the horse. Was she even with the horse? How did she manage her escape? Who helped her get away from this place and the horror of the mirrors? Or was she taken away? With only questions and no answers, I added the job of finding Autumn to the top of Cliff's tasks beginning immediately.

"Are you certain you want to bypass any local law enforcement?" Cliff asked.

Was I certain about that course of action? "Yes, for now."

"What about that woman you call Fan-Tom? You'd mentioned she's been a thorn in your side where Autumn is concerned."

"Keep her on your list of suspects regarding anything about the house and the property, but I don't want her to know that she's part of your investigation. I'll see what I can do via the Forest Service. But your number one priority is to find Autumn."

"Got it, but what about the horse? It must have disappeared about the same time."

Worried sick and feeling like a failure, I sighed. "It does seem that way. They must be together—that is the only assumption keeping me hopeful—but how could they have gone out the main gate without anyone seeing them?"

"I'll get back to you on that," Cliff said.

Chapter Sixteen

Martin

The Fantasy Maker had to be told. I apologized for my midnight call, but this troubling information about Autumn could not wait until morning.

"She's gone, vanished," I said, keeping the tension in my tone to a minimum.

"Are you sure, Martin?"

"Positive. The night clerk at the Inn said she took off in a taxi, crying, her suitcase in hand."

"We must do something. Our fantasy vacation participants have always had happy endings." The voice paused. "We must not ruin our record."

I gathered my thoughts. "The unplanned relationship with Ranger was a big surprise. We can't undo that."

"You're correct about that, Martin. However, from what you've reported, I think they are meant for each other."

"I agree. Because Autumn has strayed far from her itinerary, I've spent as much time as possible in close though hidden proximity with them. I've also been working on an extended plan to include Autumn's future beyond her official fantasy vacation. I know what she wants. May I proceed?"

"Of course, but first, find her. You are my only business partner and my most trusted friend, Martin. You've never let me or any of our clients down. I'm giving you complete control this time to see Autumn's vacation through to her happy ending. She must have a happy ending. I'm taking a short vacation of my own and will board my favorite ship for an east coast fall colors cruise the day after tomorrow."

"I appreciate your confidence. How much time is there before our next client's fantasy vacation begins?" Martin asked.

"Almost two months."

"Good. I'll have this one wrapped up long before that."

"You will be making all the decisions but do keep me informed."

"Bon voyage!"

I was confident I could live up to The Fantasy Maker's expectations. Though being promoted from a glorified, trusted errand boy to top executive was daunting, I liked the accompanying feeling of power.

Autumn

Sitting in the back of a taxi, I kept my phone's sound turned off to be less tempted to answer one of Ranger's calls, although the screen lit up every time a call came in. I picked up right away when I noticed the caller was Allison. I could use a friend right now after running away from my fears . . . and Ranger.

"Hi, Autumn. I have news you'll want to prepare for before you come back from New Hampshire."

"Well, hi to you too. What's the news?"

"Your father came home early, and I'm certain your mom has told him what she knows about your fantasy vacation. What do you think he'll do?"

"I don't know. Likely ground me for life. I cut my vacation short, and I'll be home in about ten minutes."

"OMG. Do you want me to come over, you know, for backup?"

"Thanks, but no thanks. Today I just want to go straight to my room and sleep."

"Your parents do know about your early arrival, yes?"

"No."

"Geez, Autumn. This could be a disaster."

"Yeah, I know, but I had to get out of there. I'll call you tomorrow and explain everything."

. . .

"Autumn? You're home early. We weren't expecting you until the day after tomorrow. Your father is anxious to see you," my mom said as soon as I walked in the front door.

"I'll bet he is," I mumbled. "I'm tired, Mother, and I don't feel well."

"You're going to feel much better after you talk with him." She grabbed my hand firmly and led me toward the sunroom.

"There she is, my disobedient, traveling daughter," Father said.

I wasn't feeling any better yet. The leopard doesn't change its spots. I saw that he held my vacation notification letter in his hand.

"Want to tell me about this?" he asked, his eyes boring holes in my head.

Feeling like I might throw up, I coached myself into taking slow, even breaths before speaking.

"I assume you've already read it. There is not much more to tell except that my book club friends were the ones who nominated me to receive that dream vacation. Allison was to go with me, but she backed out at the last minute."

"All right, then tell me about The Fantasy Maker," he said using his typical stiff and business-like tone.

"I can't. I don't know anything about her or him or if it's a company. All I know is that a man named Martin oversees each winner's vacation."

Mother jumped into this conversation. "We just

adore Martin."

"Huh?" I must be dreaming.

"After your father read the letter, he called an investigator who does work for his company, and that man was able to locate Martin. We haven't met him in person, just in a few Zoom meetings. Oh, and he asked us not to mention that we'd talked, said that was not allowed. So, I guess your father and I are now the disobedient ones in the family." Then, Mother giggled. *Who are these people?*

"We have a lot to talk about, Autumn, but first . . ." my father said as he approached me.

Father hugged me and said he was proud of me for taking on such an adventure and praised my newly found courage. I couldn't wait to tell Allison what had transpired here today in my own home. The change in my parents' personalities was remarkable and unbelievable. I hadn't completely let go of my dream theory yet.

Mother asked Louise, our cook, to bring out some tea and lemon bars. "These were really for your homecoming. And, don't get me wrong, we are delighted to see you, but you are two days early. How come?"

"It's complicated."

"Good. Tell us everything," Mother went on. "We already know that you were helping a man named Ranger design a haunted house. That's a good place to begin."

I should have been elated that I wasn't in deep trouble, but with that nagging issue out of the way, I suddenly realized how much I missed Ranger. He must have been worried sick and thinking the worst. And then there was the horse. At least I knew where she was. Or did I? All I really knew was where I'd left her.

"There is so much to tell you both, but I'm tired, and I don't feel like talking today. Tomorrow, I'll hook up my camera to the TV in our home theater and show you all the photos."

That satisfied their curiosity for now. I sipped some tea, ate a lemon bar, and then went to my room to rest. Whenever I closed my eyes, Ranger appeared. I owed him an explanation and an apology for running away. Someday, I would have the courage to do that, but today was not that day.

Ranger

I used to like being alone on the ground or in the air. Just my plane and the forest was all I needed. Then fate placed Autumn in my life, and I haven't been the same since. I called her every day, and she still doesn't answer. Currently, the only incoming calls I can expect come from Cliff. He checked in at least once a day though new information was rare. I wasn't his only client right now.

"Hey, Cliff. Got anything?" I greeted him for my daily update.

"I do. The good news is that Autumn is back home

in Cape Coral with her parents. So she is safe, maybe not happy, but definitely safe."

"I'm glad she made it home, though I'd rather she was here with me. How did you get that info?"

"I tracked down her best friend, Allison, just minutes ago. That gal sure likes to talk."

"What else have you got?"

"The horse didn't leave via the main gate. It left through a small side gate at the far northeastern corner of the fence line. That's why no one saw them leave. I assume Autumn was riding the horse, but I don't have proof of that. Oh, I almost forgot. There is a small, very old graveyard on the other side of the pond."

"Thanks. Is there anything I'm overlooking? Something more we should do?"

"I have fingerprints from a variety of areas around the barn, the house, and both of the gates. There's not much I can do with them without involving law enforcement, and they may not see all of the pranks as crimes."

"Yeah, I get that, but we need to identify those prints and check out a bunch more. I'm sure Fanny is responsible for most of the mischief, but the day will come when I must prove it. Want to come out to my cabin today or tomorrow? I'll make dinner, and you can bring a friend as well as your fingerprint kit. What do you say?"

"I'll check with my girlfriend, Lori, and get back to you. In the meantime, I could interview that woman you call Fanny."

I asked Cliff to hold off on that for a couple of days. I wanted to see what she might tell me now that Autumn was no longer here.

"You know, Cliff, there is one more thing. Snoop around and see what you can find out about a guy named Frank or Franklin Thompson. He goes by Thomas, and he's a server at the Golden Leaf Café."

"Will do. I'll call you when I have more news."

I dragged myself around day-to-day, trying to return to my pre-Autumn existence. I used to think I had a great life; it didn't seem so great now. I did enjoy being a dad to a broken red fox who now lived with me full-time. I couldn't let him die out in the wild due to his inability to run from predators or be put down by lethal injection. I knew Autumn would love to hold this furry little guy in her lap. Oh, well.

Halloween was fast approaching, and the obligation attached to that spooky night stared me in the face, even haunted me. I hoped that once the holiday was good and gone, I'd return to loving my job, my cabin, and my plane. Then I'd figure out what to do with the big old house if I was allowed to keep it.

I had my doubts that the required one-hundred visitors would show up. In that case, this whole mess would have been for nothing. I'd fantasized about Autumn and I remodeling and living in that house together. Without her . . . well, I can't think about that right now.

With the horse gone, I rarely went to the house. Autumn and I had most of the decorating finished before she left. I ran some ads for the haunted house, made flyers, and purchased lots of candy and real pumpkins. But the thought of operating the haunted house by myself was daunting. And, I would never, ever enlist Fan-Tom's help again, no matter how desperate I was. I hadn't heard from her or seen her since she sent the text about checking out the Halloween mural—AKA the weird wall of mirrors. Just as well. What did she expect to gain from that nasty prank?

Sitting on my ugly, old couch with Red on my lap— she adapted well to being a pet fox—I looked at her and said, "I fully expect the whole hallowed evening to be a complete disaster."

I wished Autumn could see us now. "Hang on," I said to Red and reached for my phone. "Here you go, buddy. Your first selfie." I held her close to my face and snapped a photo. She won't answer my calls, but she will see this picture arriving as a text message.

My spirits lifted, if only a little. I carried Red outside and let her limp around for a few minutes near our chosen spot for her potty breaks. Next on our agenda? Sleep. I used to make fun of people who let their dogs or cats sleep on their bed, and now I have a fox sleeping on mine.

Chapter Seventeen

Autumn

It had been several days since Ranger sent the selfie of himself with Red. I didn't reply, although I often looked at the photo. I'd sat through showing my parents most of the photos on my camera. They ooh'd and aah'd and asked numerous questions about the locations, plants, and animals I'd photographed.

The first time a shot of Ranger came on the screen, Mother said, "Oh, my. He's gorgeous. How did you two meet?"

I did not want to go there. But Mother insisted on a few facts. I kept them short and sweet mentioning that there'd been mechanical trouble with the large jet I was traveling on and that Ranger was also a pilot and offered to fly me the rest of the way in his plane. That seemed to satisfy her curiosity for the time being.

In hindsight, I should have invited Allison over for the showing—if her parents would allow that—because she wanted to see all the photos too. I'd put her off for a few more days, not ready for the interrogation about Ranger I knew she would put me through. Perhaps I wouldn't be so sad and miss him quite so much by then.

Another text came in. This time it was a photo of me and the horse. I felt terrible about leaving the horse at the feed store, but it was all I could think of to do. There was a hitching post in front of the entrance, so I wrapped the reins around it, began walking away, and called for a taxi. A young man working there loading bales of hay into a customer's truck called out, "You're coming back, right?"

"No." Still feeling confused and a bit stunned, I wasn't up to talking.

"What am I supposed to do with your horse?"

"Take care of her."

Not proud of those words or my decisions that afternoon, I shuddered and worried about the horse's welfare. The only person who might know what happened to her was Ranger, and I was still too embarrassed to call him. He must hate me by now. Right then, a whole new idea came to me. I still had Martin's phone number. True, my fantasy vacation had long passed, but since he and Father had some conversations not that long ago, maybe, just maybe, he would take my call.

Would he be angry with me for not completing my vacation? I'd take my chances. I tapped his number into my cell and let it ring ten times. I was about to hang up when he answered.

"Hello, Autumn. What a surprise."

"Hi, Martin. I suppose calling you now is a bit unorthodox."

"Yes, it is highly inappropriate for me to be speaking with you. Since we've already broken several of The Fantasy Maker's rules and policies, we may as well continue. What can I do for you?"

"I feel terrible for leaving early, and I would never have done that if it weren't for the shocking wall of mirrors. I panicked and ran, and now I'm worried about Ranger's horse. I left her at a feed store a few miles from the house. I hate to ask you to do anything for me at this point, I don't deserve your help, but I need to know if she is all right."

"I'll get back to you on that. Will you return to finish what you began with Ranger?"

I wasn't sure what he meant, so all I could think of to say was, "I'll give that some thought." And think, I did. Did I dare return to New Hampshire to finish the haunted house or advance the budding relationship with Ranger?

Just then, a text popped up, no words, just another photo. It was merely a shot of the barn's back wall minus the huge array of mirrors.

Ranger

Again, no response from Autumn for the last text I sent. Had she really forgotten about me already? I wasn't ready to give up on her yet. I'd continue sending photos to her phone. I'd even increase the frequency to a photo every day until midnight on November 1. Yes, that would be my cut-off date. If photos from the haunted house on Halloween night didn't get her attention, nothing would, and I'd have to face the fact that Autumn and I had no future.

The buzzing sound of my phone jarred me from my dismal thoughts. When I saw on the screen that the call came from our District Ranger's office, I cringed. A call from there was never good. Had someone obtained the news that I was harboring a wild red fox, that I'd rescued that injured deer, or missed a few days of work? Oh, heck. I couldn't solve a problem if I didn't know what it was.

"Ranger here."

"I'll be brief. The office has received several anonymous complaints recently, and I'm hoping you can shed some light on a few of them before I take any action. One of the co-workers in your area may be involved."

This wasn't just any caller. It was *the* head of our district in the White Mountain National Forest Service, Chief Zimmerman. That alone added a serious level of intensity. Where was this going? I hadn't a clue.

"Just listen, Ranger Lee, as I list a few of the

missteps—some on forestland, others on private property—taken by one of our own. Unapproved absences, theft of medical supplies and video equipment, unauthorized use of forest vehicles, ladders, tools, and paint."

I thought he might have been talking about me until he mentioned things like intimidation, harassment, and endangerment of other forest service workers on private property. The more he spoke, the more I figured these were Fan-Tom's missteps, not mine.

"I'm not sure about any theft of video equipment, but I am confident that some of the incidents on private property occurred and may have been instigated by employee Francine Thompson."

"Interesting. I'll be in touch. For now, carry on."

Carry on? How was I supposed to do that after this odd conversation? And who were the anonymous complainers who sounded more like informers? My imagination went wild. So far, my shortlist consisted of the guys at the bonfire where I last saw Autumn, Cliff, and even Martin. That man seems to be everywhere at once and knows everything that happens. I wondered if I was on the Chief's list.

Martin

After running my idea by The Fantasy Maker, even though I'd been given free rein to handle everything for a while, I sent an email to Autumn. I simply said, "I have news about the horse. Call me when you can."

My phone rang within thirty seconds.

"Martin?"

"Yes."

"Tell me everything. Where is she? Is she doing all right? Is she back at the barn?"

"Hello, Autumn. The feed store owner took your horse home with him and put a sign on the door to the store that said: *Lost your horse? Give me a call.* No one has called yet."

"Why wouldn't Ranger call and go pick up the horse?"

"Well, he doesn't go to the feed store anymore because he has no horse to feed, so he wouldn't have seen the sign."

"Yeah, that makes sense."

"One more thing, I think your father wants to take your mother on a trip to New Hampshire to see the National Forest and the Sugar Lane Inn."

"What? How do you know that?"

"Since you are no longer a Fantasy Maker client, it was recently decided that there should be no rules against communicating with you or your family. If your mother and father fly north, are you willing to come with them? Let me know as soon as possible. I have an idea that would make everyone happy, including Ranger and the horse."

I hoped Autumn would agree to travel with her parents to New Hampshire. Creating and imple-menting all the details of my idea would be fun, though not easy. I needed at least a week to put it all together.

The following day, Autumn called, agreeing to return with her parents.

"I do have a condition or two."

She spoke with such authority; I had to stifle my laughter.

"Okay. Let's hear those conditions."

"The main one is that Ranger cannot know anything about our arrival or the plan—whatever that may be. It must be kept secret. And I will need your help starting now because I have quite a few ideas about this trip and how it should play out. Could you be of assistance now through the morning after Halloween night?"

"We have much to discuss, don't we, Autumn?"

"Yes. Much to discuss and even more to do."

Ranger

Three days and counting. I had to admit that I was a nervous wreck. Originally, Fan-Tom had offered to help when October 31 arrived. I hadn't seen or heard from her since the night Autumn left, which was fine with me, though I sure needed some assistance.

Cliff had made it out to the cabin and lifted prints from my truck's door handles and glove box, as well as the freezer handle. After that, he took a sample of mine. I hadn't heard back from him, so I gave him a call. I needed results if I was ever going to put all the pranks and harassment to bed. Autumn deserved some answers, too, even if I had to deliver them through a text message.

"Hi, Ranger. Got the print results today. The good news is that you are not a wanted man."

I laughed, but Cliff did not. He was a serious guy.

"Francine was nowhere in the database, but most of the other prints on your truck and at the cabin matched many of those on the mirrors. Though helpful, that's not exactly proof. Here's the good part: Some of the prints on the mirrors were Franklin Thompson's. He's got quite a long rap sheet. And he has a sister named Francine Thompson."

Then Cliff summed up with a nutshell version of his professional opinion: "Fanny's brother helped with the graffiti, the dead flowers, and the mirrors. Fanny might have been on her own for the underwear and the love note lasagna. Either she messed with your keys or you were careless."

"That sounds like partners in crime or at least hurtful pranks."

"Sure does."

"What's the penalty for being an accomplice in the installation of mirrors?" I asked, attempting a joke.

My serious PI did not comment, but I kept talking.

"Great work, Cliff. My head is spinning as I add up all the facts. Knowing this additional information, I wonder what was in it for Thomas."

"Someday, we'll ask him. My head is spinning too, weighed down with all the favors I asked for and will need to repay someday."

"I won't forget that, Cliff. Thanks. And let me know when any of those bills come due."

"Oh, one more thing about your uncle. I retraced my steps through the northeastern gate and around the pond and took a closer inspection of the small grave-yard. One spot appeared to be recently disturbed, and there was a tiny headstone looking almost new."

"Don't keep me waiting on this, Cliff. What words were on the stone?"

"It said, Here lies a little bit of Robert: Leeve him alone! And leave was spelled l-e-e-v-e."

"That's about all I can take in tonight, Cliff. Thanks again."

I dissected the message as best I could. "Recently disturbed" could mean someone was recently buried there. "A little bit of Robert" might refer to Robert's cremated ashes. Leave spelled "leeve" is either a typo or a hint at Robert's last name. It's coming together! If any of my assumptions are accurate, Robert Lee was my recently deceased uncle, and some of his ashes were buried beyond the fence line.

Exhausted, I went to bed hoping for a good night's sleep. Instead, dreams of werewolves, headless ghosts, and angry skeletons burning down my house kept waking me up most of the night.

Chapter Eighteen

Ranger

I arrived at the haunted house at 2 p.m. on Halloween afternoon to add the last-minute finishing touches. My to-do list reminded me to set out the bowls of treats, open the doors, make sure the spooky CD in the barn and the CD in the house with cute Halloween songs were ready to play, and the orange lights were all plugged in. I accomplished all this quickly. Why was I rushing around? I was ahead of schedule, and likely, only a few people would show up, if any.

With some time on my hands, I replaced rushing with pacing. How would I manage a house full, a barn full, and a yard full of strangers? I was here alone. No Autumn, not even Fan-Tom. I'd banished her from my life the day after her horrible mirror prank. Ten days later, the district reassigned her to one of the remote fire lookout stations until they finished looking deeper into her participation in various incidents.

Laughing, I turned on my phone, uploaded a photo of that station, and sent it to Autumn. This time, I added a few words: Fan-Tom's new home for the next 12 months!

At 4 p.m., I opened the front gate and tied black and orange balloons on each panel, then parked my truck off to the side as an example of where people should park their vehicles. Now all I needed was one-hundred visitors. It would soon be showtime, the witching hour, the devil's playground, or nothing at all.

I was ready. As I waited for any guests to arrive, I tried not to think about Autumn or miss her, but I failed miserably. I saw her in every room, in every pumpkin, and in every decorative item she'd placed here.

It was time to put on my Halloween costume. I sighed with relief. Surely, I'd feel more relaxed hiding behind my costume. I would become a ghostly host any minute now, and I didn't mean Casper.

The loud sound of a car horn honking over and over got my attention. Looking out from the barn's front double doors, I saw two people hurrying toward me. A man and a woman holding hands, each carrying a bag.

"Cliff? Is that you?" I called out.

"Uh, Ranger, is that you?"

"Yes, it's me. I'm a ghost host tonight. I am happy to see you, but what are you doing here? Did something come up, or have you discovered any new mysteries involving this property?"

"Not really. I have a question or two I hope to answer in the near future. We're here because we thought you could use some help. My girlfriend, Lori, wants to help too. She loves Halloween. We brought costumes, in case that was required."

"Not required, but definitely appreciated."

"Great. Where should we change?"

"The barn or the house. Your choice."

They dashed toward the barn.

"We will return. FYI, Cinderella and Prince Charming will be the ones returning."

And return, they did. Then, we waited impatiently for any visitors.

"Hey, Cliff, what time is it?" His watch and his phone were readily accessible. Mine were buried under my flowing costume.

"It's 5:45."

I shook my head. All that work for nothing. "No one is coming." Not one little goblin or pumpkin or witch had come through the gate. Maybe it was for the best. Still, I had let myself dream that I could live here with Autumn someday if I did indeed inherit the house.

Cinderella spoke up. "Don't give up yet. Let's wait a while longer. Some folks trick-or-treat later than others. And, if by 7:30 no one shows, we will have our own Halloween party. I'm not letting my costume go to waste."

I looked at Cliff, then shrugged. "Sounds good to me."

Tired of standing, ready to welcome our Halloween guests, the three of us decided to sit side-by-side on the haunted house's front steps. One ghost, one princess, and a handsome prince passed a bowl of candy back and forth as we waited and waited for guests. It was nearly time to give up and close up shop.

"I must be losing my mind. Do you hear that?" I asked.

Cinderella thought she heard distant screeching and howling. Cliff said he heard the sound of kazoos and drumbeats. I heard a horse whinnying.

"A horse? Maybe my horse? No, that isn't possible. This is all too weird. Someone is playing a trick."

The three of us stood and stared at the gate. The odd combination of sounds grew louder, but still, there was nothing to see. Slowly, cautiously we took a few steps closer.

A horse walked through the gate. A horse with a rider. That explained the whinnying. It headed straight toward us. Oh, my gosh. That was my horse, but who was the rider? Darkness had arrived, so all I could see for sure was the rider wore a long flowing red cape with a hood and a mask over its eyes.

On either side of my horse walked two adults dressed as Sonny and Cher, I think. Those two were a little before my time. They were followed by dozens of costumed visitors—children and adults—all contributing to the noises of the night in what appeared to be a Halloween parade. The horse galloped toward Cinderella, the prince, and me, and then proceeded to trot circles around us. Little Red Riding Hood sure knew how to ride.

The other guests formed a half-circle in front of us and continued with their sound effects. So much for no one showing up. Instead of a few trick-or-treaters straggling in, it seemed they marched in all at once in an organized group. This mixed bag of joy and confusion left me speechless.

Cliff stepped in and said, "Welcome everyone, young and old, to Ranger's haunted house. Make yourself at home. We suggest kids under ten years old stick to the main house. The back end of the barn is super scary. Enter at your own risk."

"Way to go, man," I praised Cliff. "You were a total ringmaster. Thanks."

The crowd scattered. I noticed that Cliff headed for the scary barn while Cinderella went to greet those entering the haunted house for children. I stood staring at my horse, its rider, and the two adults I did not know.

I stepped closer to the gentleman first and held out my hand. "I'm Ranger Lee. Thanks for coming."

The man nodded and shook my hand. "I'm William, and this is my wife, Elena. Hmm. You must be Autumn's ghost." Then, he laughed.

I had no response to that confusing comment. Was

he referring to the season and the holiday? I was a ghost, and it was autumn.

The rider finally spoke, "I'd like you to meet my horse, Midnight Star."

Who was this woman riding my horse and speaking with a British accent?

"That's a nice name, but she's my horse," I said, rubbing the mare's long nose. "I missed you almost as much as I missed—"

"Oh, dear. I thought she was *our* horse." The rider removed her hood, her mask, and then discontinued her British accent.

"Autumn, you're here?" Now I know what it feels like to be in shock.

"Yes, it's me and my parents, and Martin is around here somewhere. Could you give me a hand? It isn't easy to dismount while wearing this long cape. That's why Little Red Riding Hood never rode a horse."

I stammered and stumbled like a teen on his first date. Rip Van Winkle couldn't have been more confused than I was right now. I was shocked by the plans Autumn, her family, and The Fantasy Maker's right-hand man had created.

"I thought you weren't a horsewoman," I said as I helped her down from the horse.

"I wasn't, but I took some riding lessons after we'd come up with the parade idea. I have a request. Could you please take off your ghostly mask?"

"Sure. Anything for you, Autumn." I was happy to remove the mask.

She reached up, held my face with her delicate hands, and kissed me.

"Your parents are just a few feet away," I whispered.

"I know. Isn't that wonderful? I'll explain everything later tonight unless you have other plans."

"No plans until tomorrow. Then I'll be cleaning up, shutting down the place, and waiting for the courier who will determine if I met the requirements to inherit this property."

I watched and listened as Autumn instructed her parents to find the guest book and make sure every man, woman, and child signed it.

"If that doesn't meet the 100 visitors requirement, we'll round up a few more guests," Elena added.

I walked with Autumn—or should I call her by her costume's name?—to show her all the finishing touches and reintroduce her to Cliff and his girlfriend, Lori. I had a feeling the four of us might eventually be good friends, even though one of us would be a long-distance friend.

"It's just how I imagined. You pulled it off well, Ranger. There is something for everyone. I hear sounds of delight coming from all of your Halloween guests."

We strolled the property hand in hand, keeping to the lighted areas and avoiding the back of the barn, thinking it might trigger a fearful reaction. I did not want to remind Autumn of that wicked wall of mirrors.

"Will you be taking photos tonight?" I asked.

"Does your horse eat hay?" she said with a hint of sarcasm and a cheeky smile.

Before I could answer, Autumn's camera was pointed right at me, and I heard the faint sound of the shutter clicking. I'd just been photographed.

"Hey, Ranger," said a voice from behind me. I turned and saw that the feed store owner had shown up with his kids. "We wouldn't miss this for the world. By the way, you've got a great horse there."

"I agree, but how do you know that?"

"One of my workers found the horse tied to the hitching post out front of the store. Long story short, she spent a couple of weeks at my small ranch. You know, Ranger, I don't think I've ever met your girlfriend."

"Sorry. Autumn, this is Guy Renfro. Guy, meet Autumn Reed. Or should I say Little Red Riding Hood?" We all laughed. "What do I owe you for boarding my horse?"

"Nothing. Your money is no good, except when you purchase more hay and alfalfa from me. Besides, caring for the horse and rounding up a bunch of locals to show up here tonight was the most fun I've had in years."

"Come on, Dad. You said we'd go inside the haunted house," his children coaxed enthusiastically.

"Gotta go." He followed his family to the main house.

. . .

By 9:30 p.m., all the guests were gone. Only Cliff, Lori, Elena, William, Martin, Autumn, and I remained.

William offered to donate money to Martin and The Fantasy Maker for all their creative and challenging work.

Autumn's mother added, "We're especially thankful for making our daughter so happy."

Of course, he turned them down but thanked them for the offering.

"By the way, are you ever going to reveal who your employer, The Fantasy Maker, actually is?" Autumn asked.

Though Martin's answer was brief, it came with a smile. "Probably not."

As the moon rose high above the trees, lighting the land we stood on, the air was still, and so were we. The lonely hoot of a distant owl enhanced the silence—a perfect ending for a perfect Halloween.

Chapter Nineteen

Ranger

After the haunted house had been cleared out and cleaned up some, William and Elena excused themselves and said they'd be heading back to the Sugar Lane Inn fairly soon. A few minutes later, I was shocked to see them walking out the gate without Autumn.

"Did you drive yourself here tonight?" I asked Autumn as we stood near the barn watching her parents leave.

"No." Autumn grabbed her cell phone and began tapping on the screen. "Hey, Mother. Did you forget something? I'm still here."

I listened to her side of the phone conversation, which didn't tell me much. I watched as Autumn clicked the End button on her cell and then she looked at me, dismayed.

"How did your mom reply?"

"Well, she said, and I quote, 'We're tired and need to get some sleep. We thought maybe you could stay with Ranger tonight at his cute little cabin.'"

Autumn looked up to me with her beautiful, questioning eyes. "Is that okay with you?"

"Darlin', that is more than okay. I want to spend every minute with you until you head back to Florida. With Halloween over and Fan-Tom stranded at a distant fire lookout station, we can focus on us. Let's lock up, say goodnight to Midnight Star, and go home."

Autumn

By the time we reached the cabin, clouds had rolled in, dimming the moonlight. The sky grew darker by the minute. I'd miss this rustic little cabin and was afraid I might never be here again. Sadness washed over me.

Back in Cape Coral after my parents came to their senses, I told them all about the cabin and the adventures Ranger and I had during our short time together. From that day on, they spoke of wanting to meet him and visit the cabin someday.

Walking up the cabin's steps, three frost-covered pumpkins caught my eye. One large, one medium, and one small. The sight of them brought back a joyful feeling.

"Why three?" I asked.

"That's my Halloween family. Me and you."

"But there are three."

"You're right. Let's go inside."

Ranger opened the door for me and I walked in ahead of him. What I saw next thrilled me.

"Red!" I said as she hobbled toward me, her tail wagging wildly. "You're still here?"

"That's right. She's here to stay, but that is a story for another time."

I noticed she had become a three-legged fox with a banged-up eye. Red sat on my lap, and together, we watched Ranger build a fire. Before long, he joined us.

"All set. Now tell me more."

"Father was angry until he found the letter from The Fantasy Maker. At first, according to Mother, he freaked out, forbidding any involvement with someone called The Fantasy Maker. He hired a PI who was able to track down a phone number that was answered by Martin. They talked, hit it off, and the rest is history."

Ranger put his arm around my shoulders and patted Red's head. "Your recent history sounds unbelievable, like a miracle. All that time, I thought you were so mad at me for all the crazy things that happened, you'd never speak to me again."

"I was afraid to face you after running away and not communicating. And then there was your friend Fan-Tom."

"Not a friend, a mere co-worker that most of the

crew, including myself, barely tolerated. Her employment will soon be terminated."

"Good. Even so, I never blamed you for her actions. We had almost everything lined up for my return and Halloween night planned, but I didn't agree 100 percent until I became aware of the fire lookout station and its newest occupant. Then it was all systems go—in a hurry."

"Everything about tonight was a huge surprise, the best surprise of my life. Thank you for all that you did."

"I had a lot of help from Mother and Father and Martin. It was nice of Cliff and Lori to help tonight too."

When Ranger asked if I'd like a glass of wine before we opened up the sofa bed, I quickly answered yes. That is when it dawned on me. My only piece of luggage was back at the Sugar Lane Inn. I had nothing here to wear. Ranger must have read my mind. He hustled to the bedroom and when he returned, he tossed me a Forest Service T-shirt.

Finally, we settled in on the sofa bed, sipping the wine, sitting with our legs under the covers and Red between us. I knew I couldn't stay awake much longer, but the buzz of my cell phone announcing an incoming text jarred me to a higher alertness.

It was from my father. It read: *Martin has worked his magic once again. He applied in person for several grad programs for you. Long story short, you've been accepted at one in New Hampshire, one in southern FL, and one in between. More details to follow. Something to think about. Tell Ranger he reached* 100 *guests. Sweet dreams.*

"Well? What does it say?" Ranger asked.

I read the words out loud to him. I could tell he was hoping for a specific answer. I knew where I wanted to be—as close to Ranger as possible—but there was work to do before finalizing my choice.

"You have plenty of time to work out your grad school details."

"And you, Ranger, will be the owner of a haunted house sometime tomorrow."

"Overwhelming, huh? What do you say to snuggling up with me and getting some rest?"

"I like the way you think."

Red moved to the floor and curled up in front of the fire. Ranger and I cuddled up like flexible spoons, all warm and cozy. We drifted off to sleep to the delicate sounds of raindrops tapping on the cabin's tin roof and the faint, lonely howling of wolves in the distance.

Shadows of a thousand years rise again unseen.
Voices whisper in the trees,
Tonight is Halloween! -- Dexter Kozen

A Note From The Author

My childhood home was located six miles west of Estes Park, Colorado, and 8,450+ feet above sea level. If I took a few steps from my back door, I'd be in The Rocky Mountain National Park. I took those steps often. Growing up, I was a mountain-forest girl, though I didn't appreciate the isolation and the beauty of my surroundings until I moved away to attend college in the flatlands.

Fall was and still is my favorite season. Two of my sons (I have four) were born in New England. It didn't take me long to become enthralled with its charm and the exquisite fall colors that set the sky a-blazing. I knew someday that breathtaking location would appear in one of my books. Well, someday arrived, and so did ***Autumn's Ghost***, a contemporary romantic mystery set in New Hampshire in October.

Like Autumn, I had strict parents too. Though we each resisted our circumstances, I rebelled and sought independence sooner than she did. Other than that, we had little in common. She was born with a silver spoon in her mouth . . . I was not. Photography was her passion. Mine was writing. She fell for a forest ranger. Me? A cowboy.

May your Fall months be filled with pumpkin pies, warm cider, colorful leaves, and friendly ghosts. Thank you for reading *Autumn's Ghost*. I hope you enjoyed the experience.

Cricket

What's Next?

**More standalone stories in
The Fantasy Maker Series.**

WINTER'S BLUSH
The Fantasy Maker strikes an agreement with Clay.
What's the catch? He must pretend to be someone he's
not. A quick read that includes mountain hiking, rescue
dogs, danger, and yes, some romance.

SUMMER'S ISLAND
JD won a contest and ended up on a deserted island
somewhere in Micronesia.
This is a wild beach adventure complete with danger,
love, and a dog named Noodles.

Thank You!

Thank you for reading *Autumn's Ghost.*

Would you like to know when Cricket's next book is available? That's easy. Sign up for Cricket's (almost) monthly NEWSLETTER and you'll receive notifications of new books, giveaways, and other exclusive content. https://www.cricketrohman.org

If you enjoyed this story, please leave a REVIEW on Goodreads, Bookbub, or your favorite online retailer.

Reviews are helpful to readers and appreciated by authors.

About the Author

Cricket Rohman grew up in Estes Park, Colorado and spent her formative years among deer, coyotes, and fields of beautiful blue columbine. After retiring from a career in education, she became a full-time author writing contemporary fiction and western series and sagas about teachers, cowboys, dogs, lovers, and creative women inventing unique careers—just to mention a few.

**Cricket loves to hear from readers.
Connect with her via:**

Website https://www.cricketrohman.org

Facebook https://facebook.com/CricketRohmanAuthor

Twitter https://twitter.com/CricketRohman

Bookbub https://www.bookbub.com/authors/cricket-rohman

www.goodreads.com/author/show/112683.
Cricket_Rohman

Email cricketrohman@gmail.com

MORE BOOKS BY CRICKET ROHMAN

You will find the links and excerpts for all of Cricket
Rohman's books
https://www.cricketrohman.org

The Fantasy Maker Series
Contemporary Adventures

SUMMER'S ISLAND
JD won a contest and ended up on a deserted island
somewhere in Micronesia.
This is a wild beach adventure complete with danger,
love, and a dog named Noodles.

AUTUMN'S GHOST
When Ranger learns of his odd inheritance, he enlists
Autumn's help to create a haunted house. October in
New Hampshire is gorgeous, fun and games for sure,
but evil lurks.

WINTER'S BLUSH
The Fantasy Maker strikes an agreement with Clay.
What's the catch? He must pretend to be someone he's
not. A quick read that includes mountain hiking, rescue
dogs, danger, and yes, some romance.

The McAllister Brothers Series
Romantic Western Adventures

COLORADO TAKEDOWN Book 1
This twisty cowboy adventure includes treachery
new love, family, courage, and amazing ranch animals.

MONTANA COUNTDOWN Book 2
A wealthy rancher's story-telling tendency entices two
eavesdroppers—a greedy criminal and a would-be
novelist—to venture to his Montana ranch to search for
his hidden treasure.

WYOMING SUNDOWN Book 3
Clint McAllister's challenge put his sons in grave
danger. Alice is furious about his foolish plan.
It was almost Christmas, a bad time for such nonsense.

WILD WEDDINGS Book 4
Family, fate, and formidable danger make loving and
laughing a challenge.
Trace and Troy love two city gals. Their love is strong
but their plan for new ranches and happy lives is
threatened at every turn. Who wishes them harm?

The Creative Hearts Sweet Romance Series
Creative Women Standalone Novellas

PHOEBE'S PHOTO FETISH

Phoebe Foxglove had three loves: Photography, Flowers, and Bobby.
Two out of the three served her well.

TINA'S TASTY TOURS
Tina has an impossible dream that comes with a substantial price tag. In the meantime, she works at the Punk Patio and a 1960s diner where she is required to look like Marilyn Monroe.

CAITLIN'S COW WASH
Caitlin feels trapped and out of place living in an old-fashion Leave It To Beaver household. Then, a perfect, win-win solution comes along—a cowboy named Cooper.

ANNA'S ANIMAL HOUSE
Desert gal ends up with a Pacific Northwest ranch where animals flock to her. She's a fish out of water but learns to cope, even thrive, in spite of an ongoing feud with the handsome veterinarian.

The Lindsey Lark Series
Fiction with Elements of Romance & Mystery

WANTED: AN HONEST MAN Book 1
Lindsey, a kinder teacher in survival mode after an unthinkable divorce, is brilliant in the classroom. Unfortunately, unwanted sinister challenges invade her

off-hours.

LETTERS, LOVERS, & LIES Book 2
Jake and Lindsey are in love, but so much stands in their way.
Fortunately, they are smart, multi-talented, and they love to laugh. Wendell, the 180-pound lovable mastiff, is featured throughout this series.

HIT THE ROAD, JAKE! Book 3
Thrilling, romantic, and sprinkled with humor, this novel reinvents the 'buddy movie' concept with the written word... and a pretty woman. As Jake and Lindsey travel from Tucson to Estes Park in their RV, the dangers they face become deadly.

Saving Madeline
Standalone Contemporary Fiction
An entertaining story with humor, emotion, and an unusual mother-daughter relationship.
Audiobook available too.

Christmas in the North Woods
A Children's Picture Book
Oliver Owl introduces the reader to his forest friends who are busy rehearsing for the annual Christmas Song Contest.
Audiobook available too.